T0349361

THE BOOK OF PRAGUE

THE BOOK
OF
PRAGUE

EDITED BY
IVANA MYŠKOVÁ & JAN ZIKMUND

SERIES EDITED BY
DAVID SUE

First published in Great Britain in 2023 by Comma Press.
www.commapress.co.uk

A CIP catalogue record of this book is available from the British Library.

ISBN-10: 1912697785
ISBN-13: 978-1912697786

The publisher gratefully acknowledges the support of Arts Council England.

Supported using public funding by
ARTS COUNCIL
ENGLAND

Supported by the Czech Literary Centre and the Moravian Library

Contents

CONTENTS

Introduction

I

IF YOU ARRIVE IN Prague by train at the main station and head
from the platform to the Art Nouveau cafe named after the
architect Josef Fanta, look up above the entrance and you will
see two scantily clad female statues guarding the enwreathed
Latin inscription *Praga mater urbium* – Prague, Mother of
Cities. Today this might seem like a rather pompous boast, but
centuries ago that was not the case. In the 14th century, during
the reign of the Holy Roman Emperor and King of Bohemia
Charles IV, Prague became one of the most important cities in
Christian Europe and the political and cultural centre of the
Holy Roman Empire for several decades. With its population
of 60,000, the renaissance Prague of Rudolf II was larger than
Berlin, Vienna or Nuremberg.

The current appearance of Prague's Old Town began to
take shape in the Middle Ages and, with a few exceptions, has
retained its original architecture and character. The city's
highlights include the Old Town Square, the gothic Charles
Bridge, the winding lanes and hidden corners of the Malá
Strana, the lavish halls of Prague Castle, the Strahov Monastery
and below it the Petřín Gardens with their fresh scent in
spring, and Letná Hill above the Vltava with its breathtaking
views of the vibrant city. 'Prague never lets go of you. This dear

little mother has sharp claws,' wrote Franz Kafka in a letter to a friend. And Prague does indeed have the power to seduce, enthral, caress and wound – and all of this with such intensity that entire generations of Czech and international writers have been unable to stop writing about it, even if they wanted to...

However, the city almost lost its iconic historical centre. At the end of the 1930s, Czechoslovakia was slowly preparing for war with an aggressively expanding Germany. Hostilities were averted through the controversial Munich Agreement of autumn 1938 – the leaders of Great Britain, France and Italy met with Adolf Hitler in an attempt to avoid another European conflagration and instructed Czechoslovakia to cede a significant part of its territory to Germany. The Czechoslovak president, Edvard Beneš, was faced with a dilemma: either humbly submit to this harsh ultimatum or enter into an unequal conflict without the support of the Western allies. The nation was ready to defend itself, but Beneš took fright – he was terrified at the thought of Germany's Luftwaffe bombers pulverising Prague and other Czech cities, and in the end he chose the first option.

Soon afterwards, Hitler was waving victoriously from the windows of Prague Castle, while for the Czechoslovak nation the legacy of the Second World War, apart from bitter memories of the Nazi occupation, was the trauma caused by President Beneš's ignominious decision not to defend the country. This is a trauma which still resonates today, as can be seen in one of the stories in this anthology, 'Waiting for Patrik', by the contemporary writer Veronika Bendová. When the protagonist looks out over the Old Town at the end of the story, she cannot help but reflect on what was far from being one of the finest hours in Czechoslovak history:

'And it strikes me again, when I look across the river at Prague, that all of this beauty is here because war didn't pass through this way [...] because we were cowards; because in 1938 we didn't defend ourselves and we let the Germans occupy us, because if we had defended ourselves, none of this would have been left standing...'

The alternative title for this story was 'The Reward of Cowardice' because Prague can indeed be viewed as a kind of compensation for a lack of courage. The country laid down its arms, but it held on to the magical city admired by tourists from around the world.

Although Czechoslovakia never officially entered the war, the German occupants were harassed by the resistance. In 1942 Jozef Gabčík and Jan Kubiš travelled to Prague to assassinate one of the most powerful men in the Third Reich and one of the architects of the Holocaust, Reinhard Heydrich, before they died in a shootout with the Nazis in the crypt of the Saints Cyril and Methodius Cathedral. Operation Anthropoid, as their mission was named, was even made into a British film starring Cillian Murphy and Jamie Dornan in 2016. The Czechoslovak pilots of the RAF also covered themselves in glory, though those who survived the war and returned to their liberated country were in for a nasty surprise.

The postwar freedom lasted only three years – in 1948 the Communists seized power and installed a harsh form of totalitarianism. Instead of renewing its contacts with Western Europe, Czechoslovakia became a satellite state of the Soviet Union. The former RAF pilots were suddenly seen as traitors; as they had fought for the British army (now an enemy force), many of them were faced with imprisonment and the drudgery of the uranium mines. Other opponents of the regime also suffered persecution: members of non-Communist political parties, entrepreneurs, priests, intellectuals and others who refused to adhere to the slogan 'With the Soviet Union for all time!'

The atmosphere of those early years after the Communist coup is captured in Jan Zábrana's short story 'A Memory', set in Prague in 1952. At that time both of Zábrana's parents were political prisoners: his mother Jiřina – a teacher, activist and member of the Czechoslovak Women's Movement – was sent to prison by the Communists on trumped-up charges for eighteen years, his father Emmanuel for ten years. The regime then confiscated the family's property from the essentially orphaned Zábrana and also prevented him from completing his studies, so that in the early 1950s he had to take on whatever menial jobs he could find.

His story describes the brief and bizarre experience of being employed in an abattoir in Prague's Smíchov district, where he worked alongside a former RAF mechanic who had ended up in prison twice since 1948. His wife and child were still in Britain. As Zábrana remarked, 'Never before or since have I come across a man who would curse the regime so maniacally and furiously as this ex-RAF man. "Cancer, venereal diseases and communism are the three worst scourges of mankind," he used to say, expecting to be collared for a third time any day.' After the horrors of the Nazi occupation, the 1950s did not bring much relief.

Czechoslovakia did not succeed in freeing itself from Soviet influence until the end of 1989, when the Communist regime was swept away by the peaceful Velvet Revolution. The return to democracy brought with it many forms of freedom: freedom of speech, freedom of travel and freedom of trade. Prague was deluged by international firms, tourists, foreign students and immigrants, mainly from the West, who were attracted to the city. Several of the North American, British and Irish translators who contributed to this book also came to Prague (or Brno, the second largest city in the Czech Republic) in the 1990s, learned Czech, and in some cases settled permanently in this country.

Nevertheless, the transition from a totalitarian regime to a democracy, and from a planned economy to a free market one, did not always go smoothly. Alongside many positive changes, the post-revolution period also featured the break-up of Czechoslovakia, the mafia, political corruption and the scandals surrounding the privatisation of state companies. Some of the darker aspects of these wild years are mentioned in Marek Šindelka's 'Realities' and Patrik Banga's 'Žižkovite'.

The narrator in Šindelka's story describes the 1990s as an arena of 'drunken businessmen' and 'spotty politicians' leading unscrupulous, unrestrained, cocaine-fuelled lifestyles. Banga, perhaps the most famous Czech Romany writer, recalls growing up in what was then the rough Prague district of Žižkov, where he not only had to contend with attacks by skinheads but also repression from the police and at school. The Czech Republic has still failed to make good on some of its post-revolution promises, such as improving the position of the Roma within society.

II

When Jan Zábrana quit his job at the abattoir in the spring of 1952 in a fit of anger, he went to the waterfront to cool off. In those days another gifted writer, Marie Stryjová, also used to go down to the River Vltava. Although they were the same age, they apparently didn't know each other, so they are meeting for the first time in the pages of this book. Zábrana went on to become an excellent translator from English and Russian, but he did not live to see the end of Communism and some of his writings were only brought out after his death. Stryjová did not publish any books at all during her lifetime. She committed suicide in 1977, at the age of 46, and it is only recently that the Czech literary community has begun to discover her sensitively written, psychological prose works.

Her story 'Blue' depicts an awkward date between two students one early evening in May on the Vltava island of Štvanice. The author's alter-ego, a female student called Styrová, seems to experience the greatest loneliness when she is with another person, rather than when she is alone. What takes place between the lovers is a kind of sophisticated game of love, with pain considerately minimised and unspoken drama bubbling up behind the words. The reader realises before the young man that this relationship will never come to fruition.

Perched on a hill above the Vltava is the majestic Prague Castle. The reader will be guided through one of the largest castle complexes in the world by the writer Michal Ajvaz, an admirer of Franz Kafka, Julien Gracq and Marcel Proust. In his story 'A Summer Night', the protagonist is ambushed near St. Vitus Cathedral by an eight-foot long clam, which pursues him all the way from the Castle to Malostranské Square. When it becomes apparent that he is not safe from it even aboard a tram, he remarks in surprise:

'In all the years I'd been wandering about Prague lost in thoughts of phenomenology, surrealism, Hegel and Malá Strana dandyism, I'd often asked myself: where will all this end? I'd reckoned with all kinds of things, from terrible defeats to brilliant victories, but the possibility of being devoured by a clam on the night tram had never occurred to me.'

Perhaps this absurd sea monster is a legacy from Franz Kafka, arising from his imaginings and woven together in one of the little houses belonging to the alchemists of Emperor Rudolph II in the Golden Lane at Prague Castle, where Kafka used to go to write after work at his office. Or might this creature, so menacing and yet so ludicrously out of place in the streets of Prague, be a representation of our fear attacking our common sense?

The character of Prague's historic districts has changed over time. Expensive housing and intensive tourism have forced the original inhabitants out of the centre and into the outskirts. This trend is even noted by the pickpocket Kostya in Simona Bohatá's story 'Everyone Has Their Reasons'. After returning from several years in prison, he walks through the crowded Malá Strana, wearily forging a way through 'the masses of people walking up and down like a carnival procession' and recalling the days when Nerudova, the picturesque street leading up to Prague Castle, 'was empty and instead of tourists it was just garbage men and pious old ladies who woke at the crack of dawn to make their way to St. Benedict's.' When even a trip to Žižkov in search of an old flame fails to lift Kostya's spirits, his last hope of giving meaning to his life lies, paradoxically, in going back to the jail he was released from a few days earlier.

In the anthology the reader will also come across buildings that might not be as famous and glamorous as Prague Castle or the Charles Bridge but have an equally important place in the history of the city's architecture. In Marek Šindelka's short story, we encounter the Nusle Bridge, which spans an inhabited valley rather than a river. For residents of Prague, this concrete bridge with a metro line running through it is associated with suicides. Since the bridge was opened in 1973, around 300 people have taken their lives by jumping into the valley below. Because the original safety railing was not difficult to get across, it has gradually been raised, and eventually it was topped with an additional structure made of slippery sheet metal that even climbers were unable to scale in tests.

An even more striking construction is the 216-metre-high television tower dating from the late 1980s and early 1990s, which resembles a giant space rocket. As Patrik Banga points out, a Jewish cemetery on this site was largely destroyed to make way for the tallest building in Prague – only about a third of its original area was left. And it is this surviving remnant of the cemetery that plays a vital role in Irena Dousková's story 'All's Well in the End'. In this humorous tale, the protagonist tries to fulfil his dead mother's final wish: to be laid to rest in the Jewish cemetery under the TV tower – despite the fact that it is technically impossible. Nevertheless, her desperate son does his best to come up with a solution…

Modern cities are uncompromising. Relentless urbanisation means they continually spread outwards, swallowing up their surroundings. In Šindelka's story, the narrator refers to Prague as a city 'which expands around us like a bodybuilder who's overdone it with the steroids'. As the example of the Jewish cemetery illustrates, almost anything can fall victim to progress. In Prague, brutalist buildings are now under threat, as is the old railway bridge below the historical fortress of Vyšehrad. A number of writers have joined the ongoing protests against the demolition of the iconic bridge.

Sometimes it is not just individual constructions but whole districts that disappear. In the 1970s and 80s this was the fate of the Prague district of Libeň, which used to be an independent suburban municipality. Distinctive pubs, shops and residential buildings were replaced by a bus station, shopping centres and metro entrances. The illustrious writer Bohumil Hrabal recalls the old Libeň, having spent some of the best years of his life there. 'My Libeň' – one of his last short prose works to be published in an English translation – documents the demise of his beloved district, which was gradually bulldozed to the ground. In 1988 it was the turn of the house where Hrabal had written many of his books, including the novella *Closely Observed Trains*, a film adaptation of which won the 1968 Oscar for Best Foreign Language Film.

As well as presenting Prague and literature connected with the city, this anthology also showcases different approaches to the short story genre in Czech literature: from the autobiographical prose of Bohumil Hrabal and Jan Zábrana through the masterfully written dialogue penned by Marie Stryjová to Marek Šindelka's 'Realities', which is certainly not a short story in the conventional sense. Rather, it is a precipitous declaration of love to an unknown girl and at the same time a ruthlessly accurate dissection of modern society and the pathology of the digital world. The most concise story is 'The Captain's Christmas Eve' by Petr Borkovec, the current Prague Poet Laureate, who in recent times has mostly been channelling his poetic skills into prose. It only took him a thousand words to smoothly narrate an engaging story in the otherwise unappealing setting of a retirement home.

Given that Czech is a 'minor' language which, for example, is only taught at a handful of universities in Great Britain, it is worth appreciating the fact that each of the ten stories has been translated by a different translator (or translating couple). Thanks to them, *The Book of Prague* is not just a literary excursion to a jewel of a city in the heart of Europe, but also an encouraging reminder that Czech literature still has a strong foundation in the English-speaking world.

Jan Zikmund & Ivana Myšková, 2023
Translated by Graeme & Suzanne Dibble

Everyone Has Their Reasons

Simona Bohatá

Translated by Alžběta Belánová

'CHECK EVERYTHING OVER AND then sign…but I don't need to tell you that, Mr. Kostečný, you know the drill,' the officer slid the small pile of junk and the form across the desk.

'Oh, Joe, why so formal, Mr. Kostečný,' smirked Kostya.

The old bastard can't help himself, can he, thought officer Josef. He felt prison officer Veleba's eyes boring into the back of his head and knew that he'd hear it again about the way he treated the prisoners. He coughed and tapped the paper with his pen:

'Sign it after you count the dough… money.'

Kostya peered into the envelope and slid it into his shirt pocket.

'I feel an undying loyalty for this institution,' he smiled from ear to ear, signed the release form and bowed with his hands resting on his chest.

'I'll take my leave, gentlemen.'

'We'll see for how long, won't we,' said officer Veleba, and he and Josef watched the ragged coat disappear behind the bars, waiting to hear the buzzer as the gate opened. They knew that the goodbyes would be loud for Kostya, and Veleba closed the window in anticipation to drown out the racket.

Josef was watching Kostya take his bow in the middle of the courtyard like a clown in a circus and he had to smile in spite of himself. He asked Veleba:

'Do you think he knows?'

'That he has cancer? For sure, he's not stupid and our doc isn't good at lying even though he tried.'

'Shouldn't he have just told him?'

'That's the doctor's business. And it still wouldn't change a thing. Kostya can't help himself, so he'll either do something and come back or he won't have enough time and he'll die on the outside. One way or another. That's why they let him out halfway on parole,' Veleba growled, 'even though he's a repeater.' He too was watching the spectacle put on by Kostya down in the courtyard and added:

'You've been here barely a year but I've been here seventeen and it's hard for me to remember the times when he wasn't here.'

Josef said nothing, watching as Kostya turned his face to the spring sun outside the gate and walked away towards the station to the rhythm of the metallic ruckus played with dishes and spoons on the bars of the prison windows. A fanfare saved for escorting out only the real superstars.

Dr. Forejt watched the same scene from the floor above and when Kostya's figure disappeared behind the chestnut alley, he opened the file and looked over the lung images. Kostya told him yesterday:

'Doc, I have a feeling we're not gonna see each other again.'

'I'd like that for you Mr. Kostečný, a nice and orderly retirement,' but Kostya laughed and added:

'I'll always be Kostya to you, doc. But I'm sure you're no dummy so you can be sure I'm not either. You don't have to explain anything to me…'

The train rumbled along the track that Kostya knew like the back of his hand. He used to go back to Prague this way every time they let him out. He couldn't even remember how many times it was and what to use to help him count. He liked trains and everything to do with them. He liked the constant motion and the smell of phenol in the air and as soon as he was done with trade school he ran away from the lumber yard to the railroad.

It was tough being a railroad worker, he recalled, his eyes caressing the track flying underneath. Good that you watered it down with the slammer, old man, otherwise you'd be a wreck by now.

He stretched his legs out and rested his hands on his chest. It was the best way of protecting his shirt pocket in case he fell asleep. When he used to work the trains, he never dared to rob anyone sleeping with their hands on their chest, even if they were out cold. Luckily, most people hung their coats all over and left their wallets in the pockets. Yeah, those were the good old days. And that's how we now know to protect our shit. You fall asleep and some bastard will come along and your money's gone in no time, thought Kostya, as his eyes stroked the passing landscape.

They were nearing Prague and Kostya's heart began beating as if he was going on a first date. Jail was worth it for this if nothing else, he thought, this beautiful homecoming. They rode through the Hostivař and Vršovice stations without stopping and his city was suddenly all around him. He pushed the window down and the Prague air filled his head and weak lungs to the point of suffocation. He watched the back alleys of houses and the hill above them and was taken aback by the new high-rises sticking out above the familiar neighbourhoods. You haven't been here for two years, Kostya. My oh my you have some catching up to do. And you also have to bring something for Standa. If it weren't for him, you'd do the whole time.

'If Mr. Rákos hadn't promised to take you under his wing, we wouldn't be able to let you out, Mr. Kostečný – we certainly don't need to remind you of that, do we…?' the Judge explained to him and he was right. He didn't have to tell him twice, Standa was pure class.

It was busy in front of the station, jam-packed. People from the trains and the metro were running in all directions, staying clear of the little packs of beggars. Junkies, the homeless, rambling suitcase wheels, shouting tour guides trying to usher their tourists into the buses parked down below the park. And drifters in sleeping bags all over the grass with a putrid stink filling the air and trash strewn all over. You're lucky you've got Standa, thought Kostya, as he strolled to the Florenc stop. He bought cheap rum and cold cuts and climbed into a tram heading through Karlín on to Libeň.

The walk exhausted him and he felt as though grains of sand were flying around his lungs making him cough. He sat down and managed to get the cough under control. He rested his head on the glass of the tram window and remembered how Karlín used to look before the flood. Karlín used to be Žižkov's twin, Kostya recalled. You couldn't work here, the locals were broke and if you reached for your wallet, you could get the shit beaten out of you from a lowlife you did time with. Yeah, back then Karlín was buzzing and he used to come here to party with girls.

He remembered that he was doing time when they were showing the flood on the TV and when the gypsies from Karlín saw rescue rafts floating through their streets, two, even three of them broke down crying. Where were they now? They certainly couldn't come back here now. It's also been a while. You're bad with remembering dates, Kostya, but you remember this. It was 2002, you were in for two pick-pocket jobs on the train to Benešov – that was exactly ten years ago now.

When they let Kostya out a year later, he ran straight to Standa. Karlín looked like it had been under a nuclear attack and seemed deserted. Even now he remembered how worried he had been that the water might have taken Standa's house and how relieved he felt when he found it, damaged but still standing and Standa in it.

Now it's all posh here, check it out, totally different, hope you can find your way, Kostya. He suddenly felt anxious wondering if their river bay under Rokytka had also changed.

The tram turned towards Palmovka but Kostya couldn't take it anymore and got off. He walked around the theatre and as he was passing the metal fence covering the crater left by Casino World, he felt nostalgic. Those were the days. Ending the party at the buffet, chatting with the ladies who had come back from working the streets, having a beer and then a cig on the riverbank and watching the sunrise over the water, tossing in the wallet from the tram job the night before.

Now the park surrounding the Libeň Chateau was landscaped and blooming and the tram stop was in a new spot. But otherwise, he recognised everything and when he walked down to the docks and smelled the river, he knew he was home.

'And how long are you on parole for?' asked Standa as he carefully tipped out the last drops of rum evenly into the two shot glasses in front of him.

'A year. But they don't need to keep an eye on me for that long,' grinned Kostya and tapped his glass against Standa's.

'What are you sayin'? That's blasphemy. You ain't that old, to be talkin' shit like that,' frowned Standa and Kostya replied:

'You're right, what's seventy-two in this day and age? Nothin'! I'm just beat, is all. I'm gonna go lie down. I'll head on over to town tomorrow and help you with the boats on the weekend.'

'You gonna go see your PO? They said you gotta or they'll lock you up again.'

'Yeah, yeah, not that I feel like it. You liked goin'?'

'No, I didn't. But then was then. I've been a good boy since the revolution, as you know.'

Kostya nodded. Standa wasn't a pickpocket like he was. He did time under the old regime for social parasitism and forbidden entrepreneurship. Haha. They arrested him for shit that he's now legally allowed to do. And that's how Standa opened up a boat repair shop behind the little house he had inherited from his mother right after the revolution. Standa's Dock Shop. The people from around the bay of course renamed it Standa's Chop Shop but he didn't care. He also didn't care that Kostya was a pickpocket and he let him stay whenever Kostya was out of jail. As if Standa was reading his mind, he asked:

'Ya' remember when you stayed here the first time?'

'I don't but it's gotta be a thousand years.'

'In '74.'

Kostya let out a whistle.

'You got a good memory,' he nodded in respect and remembered:

'I stayed here by myself once when they locked you up and they disconnected the power and water. I had to use a kerosene lamp for six months.'

'And then they locked you up, too,' added Standa and knocked back the last bit of rum. White fog broke apart the darkness sitting on the water and the first strips of morning sky became visible above Petřín Tower. Kostya began falling asleep to a wild cacophony of bowls and spoons banging on window bars ringing in his ears in a distant memory. Perhaps it was because he knew that he'd never go back there again and he'd die here, next to the river. And it wouldn't take long.

'Mr... Mr. Karel Kostečný, yes, yes...' the parole officer scrolled through Kostya's papers and Kostya looked around her office. First, he checked out her legs, but she evidently didn't appreciate that, so now his eyes ran up and down the walls instead. He stared out the window and tried to avoid the stern looks she gave him every time she turned a page. She finally said:

'Hmm,' and that was it. An Oscar-worthy performance, thought Kostya and said:

'You're new here, aren't ya'?'

'That's not any of your business, Mr…. Mr. Kostečný. You have a confirmation here to receive your pension, which you need to take to the social security office but let me remind you that due to your…ehm… lack of work experience, it's not going to be anything major. You have a place to live – well that was actually one of the conditions for your early release, wasn't it?' She shot another glance at him and Kostya nodded to have it over with as soon as possible.

'Please sign here, we've gone over everything else. You can ride public transport for free thanks to your age, you know what the conditions of the conditional release are…'

'Ha ha,' Kostya couldn't contain himself. 'Conditions of the conditional release, good one.' The parole office didn't think so though. She frowned, threw the pen down on the table and moved the paper over to Kostya.

'Sign here and you can go.'

When Kostya was leaving and said 'Godspeed,' she slammed her stamp on his file in response and it sounded like a gunshot. Straight to the heart, he smirked, and his good mood returned as soon as he was out on the street.

He rode the tram to Malostranská Square and started climbing up Nerudova Street towards the castle. He was taken aback by the masses of people walking up and down like a carnival procession. His head started spinning again and that was even before he reached the Italian embassy.

You're not used to crowds, that's all, he told himself. He wanted to sit down on the windowsill of a pastry shop but the procession of tourists shoved him almost as far back as the road. People swarmed around him like a raging river, their multilingual shouts mingling with smells Kostya didn't recognise.

The signboards of pubs and antique shops, two or three tables in front of tiny cafes right on the sidewalk, and Kostya walked around them, jostled by the hungry stream of tourists. The stream was lapping up the souvenirs, grabbing hot dogs and hot baked cakes smelling of cinnamon out of shop windows. A car as long as a wagon made its way up, honking like a carnival float. He needed to keep going, at least to the Old Castle Steps, then he would breathe a sigh of relief.

You keep forgetting how old you are, Kostya, and what you are. That's why they let you out, so you wouldn't die on them in there. Look, you're almost at the top. You'll take the Hradčany route and get some rest.

Once at the top, he paused for a moment and looked at the house and the pub, which he remembered as a dump smelling of unwashed ashtrays, a den for students skipping school, a beer and sausage pitstop for garbage men. Now it's a tourist attraction as crowds jostle under the sign of the House of Two Suns and even the air isn't for free here.

He turned his back on the street, which had changed beyond recognition, climbed up to Hradčany Square and sat down on a bench opposite the At the Swan Tavern. It used to be an ordinary pub, and now... just look at it. Well, it's a new era. Standa would scold you for complaining about being like the others, but he'd be wrong. A lot of things are better these days. It's just that sometimes you think about the days when you ran up this hill like it was nothing, when this street was empty and instead of tourists it was just garbage men and pious old ladies who woke at the crack of dawn to make their way to St. Benedict's or St. Nicholas. But what's gone is gone.

Kostya watched the droves of tourists circling the square and walking through the Gate of Matthias. Back in the day, Kostya, you'd pick them like strawberries but nowadays it's just credit cards and you can't even sell passports anymore. The times have swept away your profession like a tidal wave and your fun days are over, dear boy. A pickpocket working alone is a rare sight these days.

He got up, crossed the square and leaned on the stone wall above Kajetánka. He looked down and laughed at the clowns below squealing with excitement and taking a million pictures. Can't believe your eyes, can ya', you Japs? You don't have that back home, do ya'? But this is where I grew up. Right under that tower you're pointing at. I think it's fucking ugly but I guess it fits in here. I was born under it, right in Žižkov and lived there until they locked me up the first time.

Kostya tried to count how many years it's been since Yaya, who he lived with, kicked him out.

'I don't give a shit that you're a thief but if they catch you, don't you dare come back here.'

And so he didn't come back. Wonder what Yaya is up to now. Maybe she still lives in the same place, her building hasn't been torn down and she had a nice apartment, two rooms near Ohrada.

Kostya felt a pang of nostalgia for Žižkov. When they gave him a break, as Standa used to say, from the slammer, he used to wander all over Prague but he always steered clear of Žižkov. He didn't know why himself. Maybe he didn't want to see the big changes in his old neighbourhood and maybe he was afraid of seeing what stayed behind and lived on without him.

Now, perhaps because of Dr. Forejt's sad eyes during the X-ray and the fatigue he'd been feeling these last few months, he felt like looking at the intersection where he used to play as a boy. Wonder if the water tower and the old shooting club are still standing. And how does Prokop Valley look now? And what about the guys he used to hang out with?

He walked through the castle to the Powder Bridge and rode on over to Wenceslas Square. You miss a year and everything changes. Check out Crown Palace, ain't it a shame they ruined such a nice old buffet? All of Prague used to meet down there at the crack of dawn. Factory workers, public service officers, hookers, thieves, vagrants. Cops and cab drivers, fartskovki[1] and students. People coming home after partying all night crossed paths with people rushing to work. Yeah, Kostya, buffets are over just like pickpockets.

Kostya walked from Můstek to Jindřišská Street, passing taxi stands, new stores and passages where he used to know every crevice, every escape route in their labyrinthine hallways that a crook could use to get lost if he got into trouble. He wouldn't dare run away now even if his legs still worked. Wenceslas Square still looked the same. But it was like a child that had grown up and lived a life of its own, a life where Kostya didn't belong anymore. You're just watching from the sidelines now, Kostya, and there's still stuff to see, gotta hand it to ya', he smiled and looked at a group of girls as he smacked his lips. Sight for sore eyes. One of them turned around and stuck her tongue out at him. He did the same, waved and started walking faster to catch the tram that would take him to Olšanská Square.

Sadness and nostalgia battled inside him all the way to Žižkov. You're a crybaby, you idiot, he jokingly mocked, but it didn't help much. He got off at the Pod Křížkem stop and felt like those old farts who came back after years of living in exile and cried like little girls once they hit the ground at Ruzyně Airport. Kostya was locked up at Ruzyně Prison then and while watching a news piece about the airport, another inmate yelled out: 'Oh shit, well one Ruzyně ain't like the other, is it!' and got disciplinary punishment. Solitary confinement for the rest of the week. Couldn't even watch TV, couldn't go to the courtyard.

Memories of Ruzyně Prison amused him and he felt better. He walked up the path to Křížek but didn't recognise any of it. The water tower was gone and instead of the wild bushes and tall trees, all he saw were neat pathways, a playground and large signs with the city patting itself on the back for cleaning up so nice. They'd only left the grassy hill with flat trees as a theatre prop.

He walked down to Koněvova Street without turning around and climbed up to Ohrada. The buildings and houses all looked the same, just renovated, the stores were different but he remembered the building next to the pub right away. He pushed down on the door handle but it was locked. My oh my. They even have doorbells now. He read the names and only one was familiar. Janota Václav. Janota, Janota. Of course, Kostya, that's Venca, who you used to play cards with.

He stood by the entrance and couldn't decide whether to ring the bell when the door opened and a woman walking out asked him if he was looking for someone.

'I'm coming to see Venca Janota,' Kostya answered and quickly slid inside so that she wouldn't shut the door in his face. Everything came back to him once he was in the hallway. The railing was the same, as were the stairs, just a new coat of paint on the walls and the mailboxes were painted too. But everything else was the same. He climbed the two stories and stood in front of the door, to which he once had a key. There was an unfamiliar name on the doorbell, *Ing. Jiří Vyčítal.*

Yaya, where are you? he thought and made his way down again. It was only now that he realised that Yaya could well be dead and felt foolish. Just like the old farts at the airport.

The door below opened just a crack, the length of the safety chain, and Kostya saw a part of a face, which asked him, suspiciously:

'Are you looking for someone? Walking up and down like that?!'

'I'm looking for Venca Janota,' answered Kostya. His parole officer's face flashed in his head – he didn't want any trouble.

'And what do you want with me?' asked the voice in the crack and Kostya laughed. So that's Venca's nose sticking out between the door.

'Do you remember me, Venca? It's Kostya, I used to live here with Yaya, one floor above.'

The door closed. Well that was quick, thought Kostya and turned around to leave but Venca slid the chain off the door and opened it wide.

'Well come on in, why don't you?' he threw his head back and grinned as if they only saw each other yesterday.

Venca sat Kostya down at the table, started making coffee and spoke over his shoulder:

'Karel Kostečný, Kostya. I recognised you right away. Even though it's been almost 50 years since you haven't been here. I haven't gone anywhere. My wife and I've been living here our entire lives. I got married soon after they... well once you weren't here anymore. Jarka is with the grandkids to help out so I'm all alone here... a great grandfather now....'

Kostya only half listened to the stories about the people in the building and about Venca's kids, looking around the kitchen wondering how it used to look, but he couldn't remember. He used to come by to see Venca often but it's been 50 years and they flew by like rats into the sewer, as Yaya used to say. Venca didn't remind him at all of the boy laughing in the wedding photo above the couch. He wondered if he'd recognise Yaya if he saw her on the street. Probably not.

'Do you know what happened to Yaya?' he asked Venca.

'You don't know? I thought that's why you came... Yaya died, Kostya, it's been about six months. Stroke. She was in the hospital for a bit after but it was hopeless... here, have some sugar.' He moved the sugar bowl over.

So Yaya was dead. She beat you to it, Kostya.

'Why did you think that was why I came?' he asked and Venca looked surprised.

'Well... because of Jiří.'

'Who's Jiří?' Venca ran his finger back and forth over the tablecloth. Then he looked straight at Kostya and said:

'Yaya had a son. Jiří. They let him out to visit her at the

hospital and then he was allowed to go to the funeral. We talked some and apparently his mum used to tell him that it's no wonder he's behind bars all the time, that he takes after his father. Finally, before she died, she apparently told him your name but I'm not sure whether she remembered it. She was kind of out of it by then. And I didn't ask, I felt bad...' Venca became quiet as if he regretted what he'd just said but went on:

'I guess it doesn't matter that I'm telling you. At least you know, in case Jiří ever comes to see you once they let him out.'

'And he lived here? I mean before...' Kostya didn't finish the question but didn't have to.

'Well of course. Where else? But he started getting into trouble before he even turned twenty. Deep shit in trouble all the time. Just like you, I'm telling you,' laughed Venca and Kostya smiled.

'I didn't know about him at all,' said Kostya and Venca waved his hand.

'I ain't one to judge. Yaya had her reasons and she also must have had a reason why she finally told him about you. Now I'm just kind of sorry I didn't keep my mouth shut. I didn't realise you didn't know about him...'

Kostya played with his fingers, watching his hands as if they didn't belong to him. He was quiet and Venca coughed. Kostya took the hint and said:

'Thanks for the coffee... and for everything.'

Venca inhaled as if he wanted to add something but then deflated like a balloon. Before Kostya left, he asked:

'Venca, do you know where he's locked up?'

'Somewhere near Kladno,' he answered and Kostya's head span. He barely made it to the sidewalk and had to lean on the side of the building once he got outside.

'Sir, are you alright? Do you want me to call an ambulance?' asked a young woman walking by who grabbed his sleeve.

'You're as white as a sheet!'

'Thank you, that's very kind of you. I just need to take my

medicine. I'll go get some water over there,' and pointed to the pub next door but she wouldn't let go and walked him all the way to the door of the pub. She yelled inside:

'This man doesn't feel well. He needs to take his medicine,' and waited until the waitress helped Kostya inside.

She sat him by the window and brought him water before taking a seat across the table. She waited for him to get the pill out and swallow it. Before getting up, she said:

'Sit as long as you need and if you want anything, I'll be behind the bar.'

Kostya watched Koněvova Street behind the glass but all he saw was the prison near Kladno that he kept coming back to over the last few years, never realising that one of the other inmates could be his son. Maybe they sat next to each other in the canteen, maybe they ran into each other in the laundry room. Maybe they called each other names, like everyone in there.

He kept coming back to when he was signing in, trying to remember the faces and names that were yelled across the courtyard. It was no use. Then he realised he couldn't even remember what Yaya's last name was and felt ashamed. Jiří Whatshisname. You have a son and he's a bandit just like you. A boy. Jesus Christ. He must be almost 50. You left him behind. But you didn't know about him at all. But if you hadn't got caught back then…

Kostya shivered. I wonder what he looks like. He tried to think of a Jiří from their floor or from the block and remembered one. That ain't him, Kostya. Sivák was a Romani and barely 30. Holy crap my son is a criminal.

Uncharacteristically, he felt shameful and heartbroken. Mostly from the fact that he was embarrassed that his son took after him. Kostya would never be able to say, guys, my son is a teacher, a train conductor, or phew! even a doctor. Who rides in one of them fancy cars and flies all over the world and they write about him in magazines. Nope, his son is mopping the floor in the slammer or shuffling back and forth between the TV room and his cell and Kostya wouldn't recognise him even if he shared a bunk with him.

For the first time in his life, Kostya felt remorse about the huge wall, built out of bad decisions, between him and those he watched, walking behind the window of the pub.

For the first time in his life, Kostya wondered what would have been if they hadn't caught him back then. But they did and then many times after that.

He never thought about what had been and always looked ahead to what was to come. He used to bum around different shelters under the old regime, worked on the track, sometimes construction, until he met Standa Rákos. And everything was a piece of cake after the turnover.[2] He always went back to Liběň after every release, just like others to whom Standa rented rooms, under the table of course. Not many came back repeatedly and recently, Standa only kept a room for Kostya.

'I don't wanna squabble over a couple of bucks. I don't have to worry about someone dicking me over and ratting me out anymore but I want my peace and quiet. You're different, we've known each other a long time and you're a good guy,' Standa had said just yesterday.

Good guy. Just yesterday Kostya wouldn't have thought twice about it. He figured he'd live out his last few months by the River Vltava. He'd shoot the shit with Standa as long as his breath would allow, he'd have a cig and if it was a good day, he'd take a stroll around the city. He'd keep his hands in his own pockets and he'd be a good boy. Had he not gone on his little tryst to Žižkov, that's how it would have gone down. But now, my dear Kostya, it's clear as day that you're gonna spend the time you have left making sure you find Jiří, no matter what. So that once they let him out, he could go to Standa. Maybe that way he won't fuck up his life so quickly.

'Well, he didn't stay away too long, did he?' prison guard Veleba said so the whole room could hear him, before swinging back on his heels and laughing. Josef looked out the window to see what the prison officer was talking about. Kostya was standing in the middle of the courtyard looking up at the windows and waiting for the guard to walk him in. Hellos, whistles, applause and laughter were echoing throughout the courtyard.

'And here was I thinking the cancer would knock some sense into him,' officer Josef said with disappointment in his voice and Veleba patted him on the shoulder:

'When you've been here as long as I have, you won't be so naive. Don't be a dreamer, these crooks don't change and sometimes they even come back on purpose. They have their reasons. Especially for the winter so I'm surprised that he's back now, in spring. He must have really pissed them off when they booked him to have been brought back so fast...'

Kostya sat on the bench in front of the doctor's office. The guard stood next to him sticking to protocol, legs apart, his thumbs hooked into his belt, dead eyes staring ahead. You look like you're made of playdough, thought Kostya as he inhaled the stench from the canteen. Ah, smells like goulash. Make sure you don't burn the rice this time, assholes, he instructed the kitchen staff in his head.

The doc really could change his pictures up a bit, these have been hanging up at least ten years and they're all faded from the sun. The floor smelled a little different, they probably changed the floor cleaner, otherwise same old, same old. You didn't take much of a break, you've been out barely a week.

'Just go for a visit, that's much better and that way you can help him once he gets out.' Standa had tried to talk Kostya out of his idea to go back to prison and Kostya didn't know how to explain that he had his reasons. Standa shook his head the whole night but finally Kostya got him to promise that when a Jiří Whatshisname showed up here by the river, Standa would give him a chance.

'OK, but if he turns out to be some crook arsehole that's doing time for grand theft, then don't even bother sending him here. And just for the record, you're nuts, Kostya,' said Standa instead of goodnight.

'I have to find out what he is and I need time for that,' replied Kostya but Standa clearly didn't understand.

But Standa didn't know what the doctor and Kostya did. That no sentence is short enough for a repeater like Kostya, to be shorter than the number of days that Kostya had left.

He packed his stuff the next morning and left as the sun was coming up, walking along the water. The river was still sleepy and was only waking up to the city's sounds. Some fishermen were sitting on the other side of the bay and their still silhouettes were reflected in the water like a wavy mirror.

Kostya wished he could just forget his entire visit with Venca and Jiří Whatshisname so that he could just focus on what's ahead like before. But you don't have much left in front of you, dear old Kostya, and some things just can't be forgotten.

He chased away the desire to go back and walked ahead along the path, breathing in the spring air, his eyes squinting at the sun. The sunrise was over and done with, having handed over the baton to another day.

Kostya stopped, sat down in the boat tied to the dock. He lit up but as soon as he inhaled, his lungs turned inside out. He threw the cigarette away, wet his hand in the river and wiped his brow. The water smelled of reeds and mud. The boat rocked back and forth like back in the day when he rowed around Žofín Island with Yaya. She wore a blue dress but he couldn't recall her face anymore. Don't be sentimental, you idiot. Angry at himself, he went back to the path and wanted to walk along the riverbank but the new buildings and fences didn't let him go any further. That's too bad. He wanted to say goodbye better.

He walked all the way to the Libeň Bridge, climbed up the

stairs and started looking around for the best spot. It's gotta be a big store with shopping carts, Kostya. If you're going back, it better be with a bang.

He crossed the street and walked into the Kotva department store. There didn't used to be a supermarket here. He stood around for a bit, looking to see where the cameras were. He also noticed that the security guard at the checkout was already on to him and was saying something into the walkie talkie on his arm. Kostya walked through the turnstile without a basket and the security guard watched him like a hawk. He used his walkie talkie again and it was clear he wouldn't let Kostya out of his sight. That's just what we need, boys, smiled Kostya as he shoved expensive wine bottles into his coat pockets and tried to be in the camera's field of vision. Make it good, Kostya, he told himself as he made his way through the store with his coat jingling. When he got to the checkout, he said out loud to the old lady waiting in line:

'Please let me through, I don't have anything…'

That's exactly what the two behind the cashier's desk were waiting for and when they frisked him and led him out, he managed to kick over a pyramid of pots and pans – the bang as they collapsed all over the floor was absolutely colossal. You're not wrong, Kostya, you're going straight back after this performance, that's for sure.

Even now, as he sat in the hallway in front of the doctor's office, he chuckled to himself and was convinced that if Standa had been there he would have laughed so hard he'd cry. And their faces when they realised that he was on probation! Priceless. But that's not why he was here.

He didn't even know if Jiří was here, let alone what he was like. Because if he were a crook doing time for grand theft or drugs, then everything would be fucked. But maybe not. Even Venca said that he was just like you and you're not that bad. If Jiří turns out alright you'll tell him everything.

Kostya kept mulling it over and waited patiently for Dr. Forejt to open the door of his office and invite him in. Forejt knows for sure that he did it on purpose, but Kostya will tell him that he just missed everyone, it's not anybody's business. Not even Doc's.

He'd find Jiří on his own and then he'd tell him everything, no bullshit. And he'd also tell him about Standa so that he had a place to go when Kostya was no longer around. But whichever way things turned out, he had his reasons for coming back. So that he could tell Yaya one day that he tried to make it right, something he didn't even know that he had screwed up in the first place. Maybe Yaya would forgive him just as he'd forgiven her.

Notes

1. Fartsovka: a slang term for the illegal purchase or resale of imported goods banned in the Eastern Block, also referring to those people involved in this illegal trade. Fartsovki were mainly young people, as well as those who had the opportunity to communicate with foreigners, such as guides, translators, taxi drivers, and prostitutes.
2. The Velvet Revolution of November 1989.

A Memory

Jan Zábrana

Translated by Julia and Peter Sherwood

IN THE SPRING OF 1952 I was out of work for the third time since being kicked out of university the previous summer. For a while, I would regularly drop in at the employment office to see what was on offer. On one occasion they even gave me a placement at the Křižík works in Karlín, but the moment I submitted the political background questionnaire they sent me packing. It was the same story elsewhere.

'Ostrava...' they'd say, if they said anything at all, 'how about going there?'

When I failed to show the requisite enthusiasm, they might add: 'Why don't you try a collective farm?' But most of the time they didn't add anything, and instead became very busy all of a sudden, or needed to dictate a letter to a secretary.

I didn't try a collective farm. I didn't feel like leaving Prague. At the end of March, in Arbes Square, I bumped into a lad I knew from Chuchle, and he gave me a tip about the Smíchov abattoir. I made my way there and what I put in the questionnaire was that my father and mother had died, which saved me from having to give my parents' place of residence (fortunately, not even in 1952 was I expected to specify the cemetery where they were buried) and I just crossed out the other columns relating to my class origins. They didn't ask any questions, said they'd take me on as a temp to begin with and that if I did well I'd be taken on permanently. They wouldn't stamp my ID with the confirmation of employment status – which I needed – but they did provide me with a temporary job certificate which was enough for the national council office in Braník to issue food stamps for April.

I was taken on as a driver's mate. We picked up meat from Prague South and delivered it to Smíchov. We were a real ragtag bunch. The driver I worked with had spent the war in England, serving as a mechanic with the RAF. He'd left a wife and child in England and had already done time twice since 1948: first twelve months, then four. Never before or since have I come across a man who would curse the regime so maniacally and furiously as this ex-RAF man. 'Cancer, venereal diseases and communism are the three worst scourges of mankind,' he used to say, expecting to be collared for a third time any day. He always had English cigarettes on him that he sold, though not to us, as we couldn't afford them. The other driver's mate, Berenda, was a lout from Smíchov, a notorious drunk, the last dinosaur of Prague's colourful lumpenproletariat, who saw himself as a wily old fox. He took the job at the abattoir because chaps in the pub had led him to believe he could steal meat from there, take it home and sell it. But they were wrong: the less the personnel department asked, the more they would frisk people at the gate and rifle through bags at the end of the day. I didn't swipe a single piece of pork crackling the whole time I worked there.

For second breakfast – provided we were at the abattoir, which we usually were not, since we were on the road at this time – we'd get fatty pork cheek, or we'd cook up some lungs.

Frankly, no one really minded how much we ate and the men would bring bread from home and stuff their faces like crazy. For the first two days my eyes were bigger than my stomach and I gorged myself on pork cheek until I nearly burst, but not being used to eating meat so early in the day I was sick each time. The next few days we were out on the road so we got no second breakfast and on the remaining days I got nothing but a bag of lungs. In the evenings I'd go hungry since I was going to be paid only after the first two weeks. There was no one I could tap up for a loan: my best friend Helmuth, who'd studied theology with me, was in the slammer, and Arturovič, a journalism student from Yugoslavia who was stupid enough to sign an anti-Tito resolution in 1950 and now couldn't return home, was so despondent that he took up with a girl he didn't really care for, just to get a full stomach. Sometimes in the evenings, when we hung around the embankment, he would curse himself in his awful, faltering Czech, calling himself a prostitute.

I went over to accounts to ask for an advance, but they said no. The butchers were better off: they got smoked meat or sausages for their second breakfast and were munching something all day long, but being butchers they looked down on us, drivers' mates. They knew what sort of rabble we were. We never got anywhere near the smoked meats.

One day we went to Příbram to pick up a consignment and on the way back Berenda tried to persuade the driver to stop so he could slice off a chunk of meat and drop it off at his brother-in-law's in Zlíchov. They argued for a while as the former British royal airman objected, determined not to end up in the slammer for a third time, but eventually, just before we reached Zbraslav, he pulled up. We got out of the car; the airman lit a Philip Morris and grabbed a pump as camouflage in case any nosy parkers drove past. I was told to stand by the side of the lorry so that my body would block as much of the words *Prague Meat Industry* as possible. Berenda took a pocketknife out of his blue overalls, flicked it open, and crawled under the tarpaulin. I heard him rummaging and grunting under the tarp as he lifted the meat and then slapped one chunk against another.

'Move it, we can't hang about here too long,' said the airman. 'And make sure you don't leave any fingerprints.'

Berenda didn't reply. I could hear him muttering to himself under the tarp.

'Shit,' he said. 'Shit, shit, shit!'

Then he jumped off the lorry, folded his knife and put it back in his pocket. Our consignment consisted of pig halves and quarters of cows, all cleaned out, gutted and in one piece, so a small decrease in weight might have passed unnoticed but even the thickest of butchers carving the meat would have seen that someone had sliced chunks off. So the theft was called off and we remained honest lads. The airman heaved a sigh of relief while Berenda was furious, though their contrasting states of mind didn't prevent them from spending the rest of the way back to Smíchov trying to outdo each other in bitching about the regime.

I barely lasted two weeks at the abattoir. It was raining on the morning of 12th April as we picked up pig halves from refrigerated carriages at the goods station. After unloading them, we had to carry the carcasses to the fridge on our backs. The pigs had come from Slovakia, the last, well-fed winter batch, and the halves were massive, nearly a hundred kilos apiece and each lorry was crammed full of them. The airman left us in the lurch. As a driver, he didn't have to do any heavy lifting: it depended on his goodwill, which he lacked. We were huffing and puffing like nobody's business. Berenda's wasted alcoholic's face swelled with purple blood. Every time I went back from the refrigerator to the lorry empty-handed my knees were trembling and tiny sparks shot left and right out of the corners of my eyes. After we had carried about five pieces each, I slipped on the stairs and half a pork carcass landed on me like a soft, fat white coffin lid. When I managed to scramble out from under the pig, I found I'd done something to my ankle; I couldn't stand properly on my left foot. The airman, who stood by the lorry smoking his Philip Morris and grinning like a mildly bored and mildly amused little Judas, nearly split his sides laughing when he saw me limping along. I called out to him and he helped me drag the half carcass, soiled with mud, from the stairs to the fridge and ram it onto a hook.

I didn't go back to the lorry for another. Instead I hobbled to the locker room, cleaned up, changed into my own clothes, and had a feel of my ankle which was beginning to swell. I didn't dare change into my flats and kept on the lace-ups I'd bought the previous year with a voucher from the Tatra factory, tying up the left shoe so firmly that the lace almost ripped. From the locker door I removed the slip of paper on which I'd written 'ZÁBRANA' in block capitals on my first day and tore it up. I put the padlock I'd brought from home in my pocket and headed for the personnel department, leaving the empty locker open, with my overalls and shoes stowed away in my bag. As I passed the two low buildings where the animals were slaughtered, through the window I spotted two Bulgarian butchers drinking raw cow's blood from a freshly slaughtered cow out of a mug, which put me off the abattoir for good. I didn't linger at the personnel department but had to return the certificate of temporary employment without which I couldn't get any food stamps. The staff in accounts tallied my days and said I should come and collect my wages on payday.

I didn't say goodbye to the airman or to Berenda. It was raining as I passed the gate. The sky above Prague was grey, the rain on that long-ago 12th of April not falling from individual clouds so much as from the entire sky, and yet the wind – I remember distinctly – carried with it a whiff of spring. The rain was gentle but persistent, having begun first thing in the morning and continuing all afternoon, stopping only at some point during the night. As I pulled my head in, I could feel my coat getting wet and my face getting cold. But my foot was hurting less and less with every step, and I sighed with relief, realising that I would be able to walk it off and that it wasn't going to be serious.

I walked down to the river, desperate for a cigarette – I had two left in a soft white packet, one broken and one crumpled, but no matches, and as it was before lunchtime, the only people I could see were women with shopping bags and children, and I had to walk along several streets before a tram pointsman on a corner gave me a light. Feeling a little dizzy, I stopped and looked around, the Prague of 1952 stretched away to my left and right and the streets were gloomy in the rain, I didn't have enough money for a tram ticket or a box of matches, I was hungry and getting soaked, the posters on the street corners tried to persuade me that life in this world was for the people, and eventually I ended up by the river again and stood there leaning against the wet concrete railing. It was midday, a loudspeaker hidden somewhere around a corner behind my back was blaring out the signature tune and the local Prague news, the speaker's voice sounding hollow and completely unintelligible, pummelled to the ground by the driving rain. I stood there leaning against the concrete and couldn't take any decisions since there weren't any decisions to be taken. At that moment I knew with absolute certainty that I had to stay faithful to the purity, the despair, the hopelessness of that spring – which would soon slip into into the distant past – when I'd foolishly assumed that life was coming to an end, that it was bound to end, just because I could not imagine how it could possibly go on.

The rain fell into the river so delicately that it left no trace on the surface of the water and was picked up and immediately carried away by the flow, there was a lot of water but it was murky and heavy, the current was slow but strong and majestic, yes, the river was alive and the city of stone on the opposite bank was dead.

I went to see Božka. She ushered me into the deserted baths, drawing back the white curtain behind me with the practised gesture of a medical orderly. The curtain swirled around me like a sheet thrown over a cadaver. I just sat there for a while, listening to her chatting with the women on the other side of the door and to the slapping of calves being massaged, and then took my shoes off, filled a bath with water and sank my throbbing ankle into it. It felt good.

Blue

Marie Stryjová

Translated by Geoffrey Chew

SOMEONE WAS KNOCKING. I put my book down.

Rom was standing at the door, coat on shoulder, wearing a pale blue checked shirt.

'Might I ask if you would fancy going for a walk? May I invite you?' he smiled, a small part of his upper gum showing.

'Come right in,' I said, walking back into the room.

He didn't come in.

I leant out of the door. 'Aren't you coming any further?' He was standing smoking at the railing in the middle of the hallway.

'I shall wait here,' he smiled.

'But it'll take a while.'

'I shall smoke another cigarette.' He tapped his coat pocket.

We headed for the tower, for the station, for the riverside. I felt at ease.

'The other day I was hobbling along here with my leg in plaster. With a walking stick, like some old lady,' I said. It seemed a long time ago. 'It was an hour to the student cafeteria and an hour and a half back.'

'Half an hour longer home because someone pleasant was in your company?' Rom shifted his shoulder, keeping his eyes ahead.

'It's well known that you are your own best companion.'

'Who was it who said that?'

We laughed quietly and said nothing.

I went on. 'No, it was the terrible food at the cafeteria that was weighing me down. Like the rocks in the wolf's belly when they sewed him up. But I seem not to have ended up in the Vltava.'

'What a loss that would have been for scholarship. Such a promising young life.'

'Or an accursed one, if you like that phrase, though it's one that comes up only in literary criticism. You won't find it in newspaper features. Life is tempestuous there.'

'Beaudiful,' he said, pronouncing the t like a d.

My life was neither turbulent nor accursed, but rather bland. The evening before Rom came had been dull. When all the girls had left the university residence, it seemed to me that absolutely everyone had gone, and I was glad at first that I could study in peace while the others were dispersing. Then I looked through the window – it was low down, above the pavement. I was living on the mezzanine floor and I wanted to be a witness of what was going on outside. Nothing was happening. The street was a short, quiet one, all stone with tall, dark, grey houses opposite. A figure walked out, and disappeared, though the girls – the girls as well as the boys – were no longer leaving, even from the residence. Beyond the figure there was a void. It was dispiriting. I was sorry about something – something I should have done but hadn't. There was something that wasn't as it should have been, but I didn't speculate about what it was.

It was late May and the exams were almost upon us. I walked away from the window and picked up a big new book from the table. I counted the number of pages I'd have to read through every day, though I wasn't obliged to study for an exam. I worked out how far in I had to get that day, switched the little table lamp on and put a pillow behind my back. Before I started reading, I let my thoughts wander aimlessly for a little while.

'I'd light up, if there's no objection,' I said, gesturing at Rom. When we were still dating, he never liked me smoking in the street. He would take my cigarette before I was able to light it, and stick it in his pocket. I'd walk round to the other side of him, and though I'd never reach into his pocket, he'd defend himself by grabbing my hands and outflanking me, remarking, 'A lady ought to walk on the right-hand side.'

I took a cigarette out of my coat pocket. Quickly, he lit a match. 'Allow me, I'll give you a light.' He leant over me.

He was very tall, with curly hair of an uncertain colour, and ample, glossy lips.

'Thanks,' I said, avoiding his gaze, and trembling.

'Are you cold?'

'No.' I shook my head.

'I'd be only too glad to lend you my coat.' He held out his coat in his hand.

I turned from one side to the other. 'I haven't walked this way for a long time.'

We had reached the bridge.

In the air over the water there hung a bright, melancholy blue, the kind that evokes sadness or discontent, that whips up loneliness, and that kindles unbelievable dreams and desires, inchoate, but glowing red-hot and stark naked.

I saw, as if for the first time, that Rom had a reddish complexion, with freckles at his neckline, and I turned my eyes away.

We had arrived at the stairs that lead down to Štvanice Island.

This was where we used to come in spring last year each time we went for a walk, no matter where we had come from or where we had been heading.

We slowed down.

'If Mademoiselle has no misgivings about me, I would like to invite her,' he said, gesturing at the island, and bowing excessively politely.

The island was green, filled with dense, dark canopies that ran under the bridge.

'I really don't know whether I should trust you,' I said, stepping down from the stairs, and breaking into a run.

He ran too, jumping to the ground.

On the bottom step I tripped. He held out his hands.

'You mustn't hurt yourself.'

'If it weren't for you, I wouldn't have been here at all.' Rom kept his hand under my elbow.

I walked along the footpath, with Rom behind, touching my elbow. I quickened my pace.

'You've never been so sweet.'

'What do you mean?'

'A crosspatch. Your thoughts are always somewhere else. Just commenting on literature. No other subject could ever be raised with you.'

I looked at him. He smiled.

'Whether Tolstoy is successful in every line he wrote or not. And whether literature forms a single current or ten different streams. Those were the only problems for which you lived. Whether literature is a common stream or whether it is the work of individual authors! And as for Tolstoy, whether his religious enthusiasm contributes to his art or detracts from it. Those were always the questions, O esteemed one!'

Now it seemed to me that all his questions had been quite off course.

The footpath petered out. We were walking on the grass.

We came to a halt at the end of the island.

'Shall we sit down?' – Rom watered down his proposal by adding, 'For a quarter of an hour.'

We sat in silence at a place where the grass ended and a barren clay slope down to the river began.

Here somewhere – perhaps a little to the right or the left – were the places we used to come to last year.

We sat down. Rom was staring ahead.

Below were the grey ripples of the Vltava.

I lit a cigarette. The air began to thicken and turn grey.

'Don't you think you smoke rather too much, Miss?' Rom broke the silence, leant on his elbow and turned to me.

'I don't *think* it at all. It's a reality. I do smoke rather too much,' I chuckled.

'After all, you made a solemn promise six months ago, as I recall, to avoid even looking at a cigarette.'

'Phooey, I don't have to look at it,' I laughed sharply through my nose.

He snatched the cigarette out of my mouth. 'Girls shouldn't be smoking too much.' And he began kissing me. I never knew whether it was a pretext or whether he really didn't want me to smoke too much. Breaking away from his interminable heavy kissing, he began scrabbling in his pockets. He lit a cigarette, said 'I owe you a cigarette,' gave it to me and lit another for himself.

'You are renowned for being strong-willed in other respects,' he added, keeping up the irony.

'Mmm,' I said, twirling the cigarette in my hand. 'One other failing…' – I didn't finish the sentence. I was no longer at ease.

Rom moved to sit closer to me.

'Do you still keep studying sixteen hours every day?'

'Only twelve,' I replied. 'My roommate chatters away for an hour before supper and another hour after supper. You've got to go to the cafeteria for your lunch – you don't have a servant to bring it to you. And on top of that, alone…' I threw a pebble into the water.

'Alone?' He touched my elbow.

'I've forgotten now what I wanted to say!' I said, laughing tensely.

I didn't turn around.

'How many pages will there be in your first book?' He sat down next to me and put his arm around my shoulder.

'You don't have the right to do that anymore,' I protested, looking at him as his mouth was searching for mine. 'We aren't dating now,' I said to his great swollen lips.

He edged away quickly. He sat a short distance from me, with his knees drawn up and with his head in his hands upon them.

I felt sorry for him.

I lit myself another cigarette. Clasping my hands around my legs, I rested my chin on my knees and gazed out at the water.

The waves on the Vltava were grey and turbid, almost dirty. They were rising up quite high but not rolling over each other. They remained standing up while new ones rose from below. Reaching their crest, they fell back.

Rom lay down.

I was throwing small stones into the water. They were splashing at the edge of the river. Rom didn't hear them.

I felt a desire to go to the water, to enter it, to submerge myself completely, to feel the waves with my hands and with my body, to feel nothing except them, to lose myself in the flow of the murmuring water.

I got up. Rom was lying down.

For a moment I stood with my hands behind my back. Rom was motionless.

I went down to the river. By the bank the surface was calm and still, except for the waves moving from the centre and the water lapping at the bank. I wet my hand in it, moved it back and forth, and dipped my arm in up to the elbow. I became afraid – Rom wasn't with me! I withdrew it and went back to the bank.

I sat down beside him, resting on the palms of my hands. Evening fell. The sky was a hard, dark, deep purplish blue, the water was rippling grey. Now and then there was a gleam in a wave, but most of the waves were grey and turbid.

Over my shoulder I glanced at Rom.

He was propping up his head on his hands, chewing on a blade of grass.

I leant over towards him. Right over towards him. His eyes couldn't be seen. They were a clear blue. I took the grass blade out of his mouth and kissed him.

He made no response.

I seated myself in my previous place.

'Could you give me an answer to just one question?' he asked, after a pause.

'Why did you kiss me?' He said it after another moment.

I had wanted him to start kissing me.

'Can I ask you another question?' He sat tearing a blade of grass into tiny pieces in his hands.

I was looking at the water.

'You don't have to answer if you don't want to' – he suddenly said one of the words in Slovak, his native language.

'Were you thinking that we would be dating each other again? That I'd come for that?'

I lay down, quickly tearing out handfuls of grass and throwing them into the river.

No, I had not been thinking anything. *He* was the one I'd already been unwilling to date. I'd have felt bothered again. It was his *existence* that disturbed me and forced me to do things I didn't want to do. When I came back from our meeting I wrote him a letter, right now, I'll write to him tomorrow morning: I justified our breakup to him in it – we aren't right for each other, we have nothing to say to each other as two *people* (if we were to bump into each other, our conversation would dry up before we knew it), as the days passed, though, I softened my decision so as not to hurt him, I apologised and was relieved I hadn't sent it to him yesterday. I counted the days until our next meeting, the day after tomorrow, well, tomorrow. I trembled, anticipating that the next evening would be *different,* and I was bidding him farewell until the last minute before his arrival and distancing myself from him.

'I was worried that you'd suffocated. You were lying there fully dressed with a pillow over your head. It's two o'clock.' Jitka was back from the cinema and she'd been down to the river bank with her colleagues and had been singing there until one o'clock.

'What on earth happened to you?'

'Nothing.' I propped myself up a little and stayed lying down. 'I've broken up with Rom.'

'We've been here before.'

'No, for good.'

'For a fortnight? A month?'

'But I really don't know how I'm going to…' I shrugged my shoulders helplessly for a long time.

'How many times have you broken up?'

'This is the third time.'

'So get on with it and sort it out quickly.'

'No.'

'Are you in love with him or not?'

'I don't know.'

'Do you know so little about yourself? And you call yourself…?'

I didn't call myself anything. I saw empty days ahead of me and they scared me. After all, hadn't I'd been alive before him, and they weren't empty then? Every evening Jitka was doggedly asking me whether I'd phoned yet.

'Off to the phone with you.'

I didn't move.

'Don't let me see you here looking like a dying duck in a thunderstorm.'

'Am I supposed to push off into the bathroom?'

'There's no need for that. You have a right to the room just as I do.'

'I'm not going to be moaning in there.' I just gave up the argument.

'You're always capable of moaning. You're as stubborn as… What's that animal called?'

'A mule.'

'If he wasn't totally crazy about you, he wouldn't be running here like some little puppy dog every time you just crook your little finger,' she said. 'How many times has he been standing outside the door with you away and gone!'

Always 'before a breakup'. Let him leave on his own. I can't send him away.

'Shall we go?' suggested Rom.

I took a long time cleaning the grass off my skirt. Rom was standing by the water.

We started walking. One thing after another.

Rom turned from the grass into the darkness. Why? I was glad. There were lamps standing in two garish yellow ranks by the path.

Under a tree, though there was no lamplight cast there, it was not completely dark. Someone was there. A figure. Lying on the ground, by a thick tree trunk, on the grass. Knees drawn up. No, it was two figures on top of one another. Rom wasn't near and I was right next to them. Two people lying on top of one another, not moving.

I averted my offended gaze from them and at the same time wanted to go back to them, to approach them, and see what they were doing. Were they having sex? But without moving? Or engaging in foreplay? Or only embracing and kissing? More than we did?

I hung my head, afraid to look at the trees. They could have been at it again next to each new tree. I was ashamed to look at Rom.

How could they do it here? Right in front of everyone? In a public place? As if it meant *nothing*! People could have been walking past, many, many people could at this moment have been walking round them. They could have startled them, defiled them with their glances. Are they not afraid of being disgraced in the eyes of strangers? Is it possible to have sex *here*? It frightened me. *Here. And now.* There, back in the darkness, it could have happened with Rom only an hour ago. And last year we were here every other evening, and on all those evenings we could have – been seen by other people?

Suddenly I noticed that it wasn't dark. The moon was shining. It was shining on the lovers. For that reason they could be seen.

It was gently lighting up the grass in front of us. The grass was dark and green, with a dull yellow light hanging over it. I moved beyond the moon. It was to the side of the island, full, pale and bright.

When I begin *living* with a man, it won't be *with Rom*. Our first evening – or night or moment, it won't be a moment, but an unceasing hour that will bring time to a halt, it will be eternal, it will be significant and awful, verging on the unbearable – will happen in a place completely cut off from people, forever secluded from them. Removed from us ourselves, from the sort of people who like the rest of us walk the streets in broad daylight, speaking in ordinary voices and feeling hunger. *There* we shall cease being those common people. And then, after *that*, when we awaken, perhaps we shall altogether cease being the kind of people we were before. It will transform us.

The moon was shining softly on the grass before us, a dark, flat lawn running into the dark under the bridge. Rom was a little distance away from me.

If only he had caressed me, if only he had just said: *Don't be afraid*. I clasped my hands inside my coat pockets.

'Would you care for a cigarette, Miss?' Rom took two steps towards me, offering me his packet of cigarettes.

'I have my own.' I pulled mine out, turned round and lit a match.

He let the match burn completely down in his hands. He tossed it on the ground.

'You forgot to light it,' I said. He kept the cigarette between his lips.

He held it in his hand.

He took a step towards me. Was he coming near? We were still in shadow.

He continued on his way.

We came to a stop by the lamps, and I looked down at the ground. It was the end of our walk. The footpath was bestrewn with dirty red sand that beat like rust into my eyes.

Was this now the end? Was he really not about to come back over to me, and weren't we about to start kissing?

He began mounting the stairs, waiting for me to come. I came.

We climbed the stairs in the same silence we used to keep while we were dating each other.

Every time we stepped out onto the bridge, either hand in hand or with Rom taking my arm, the neon lights fell upon my eyes, stinging cold and white, and pierced me with a bitter, seemingly bluish void, and I felt that what had happened down on the island, the endless, endless kissing with Rom, was ugly. I should have separated myself from him, torn myself away immediately, and run away to a place from which I would never return here again.

'Weren't you wanting to say something a moment ago?' asked Rom, halfway across the bridge.

'Perhaps. But I would rather not explain. So I don't become tiresome.'

The Captain's Christmas Eve

Petr Borkovec

Translated by Justin Quinn

I ONLY HAD FIVE months of non-combatant military service because then I got sick. It was the mid-90s, and I worked as a nurse in a Prague retirement home. I almost completely erased it from my memory. I only remember the first day on the job, and how the nurse took me from room to room: didn't knock, didn't say hello, and didn't introduce me to anyone. Just walked in, stuck her hand in the air, winked at me and roared out: 'This room's for two, but there are three here. And get a load of that stink!'

The faces of the three women slowly turned towards me as if from another world, but by then the nurse was closing the door and we walked on. She then said something in the hallway that I remember perfectly. In the years after, I occasionally and cheerfully thought about myself in these very terms; at other times, it haunted me: 'The ones who're past it – you can say what you like to them.'

And that's all I remember about the care home. Nothing else. Total blank. It almost gives me the chills.

But wait! There was Captain Kolman!

Mr. Kolman was infirm and unassuming. The title of 'Captain' gives the impression that he wore an eccentric hat or a flower in his grey lapel. Everybody just called him that. No one, I think, knew whether he was a naval captain or a football captain; in the army or the air force or the secret police. And no one thought to ask this taciturn, shy man.

He left the home only once a year, on Christmas Eve. For years, a friend would come by at 3pm and take him to a family who had Christmas dinner waiting for him. But the friend hadn't come the year before. And now they wouldn't let the Captain go alone.

'He didn't come – there's no point in waiting around for him!' the nurse told him.

'Hah! Bunkum and balderdash. Cock-and-bull stories from start to finish,' concluded the porter, as Mr. Kolman, chocolates in hand, told her the story, begging her to intercede.

It crossed no one's mind that Mr. Kolman would even think of going anywhere on Christmas Eve, let alone set out, after what had happened the previous year. So, when I suggested that I would accompany him to the family, the nurses and other caregivers were astonished, claiming that Mr. Kolman had made up the name and address, and we'd end up back at the home with nothing to show for all the effort. The head nurse wanted to forbid me from even trying.

'Kolman? He's almost past it. Are you even sure you'd be able to handle him?'

Finally, we left. At 3pm sharp. I reckoned – I remember well – that we wouldn't find it.

But Captain Kolman had the name and address – U Ladronky 1338/23 in Břevnov – written on a piece of paper. He was looking forward to it, talking, even joking, repeating several times that I'd even be able to 'find the house without his help.' But when we eventually found ourselves standing in front of the long bungalow with the right number, empty and shuttered for the winter, it turned out that maybe the street name was different, and the number too, for that matter. But Mr. Kolman was in good form and wasn't put out. We combed the adjacent streets at a leisurely pace, examining bells and gates and front gardens full of ivy. In one of the gardens a woman stood motionless, lightly dressed, looking as if she had just come out with the ashes. I wanted to ask her, but I didn't know what to say exactly. I suggested to Mr. Kolman that he should ask himself, and he did so. He began to tell the lady in detail how things were on Christmas Eve in the family we were looking for. The woman looked at him absently, and when he had finished, she asked: 'What day is today?'

'The twenty-fourth. It's Christmas Eve,' I replied.

'What time is it?'

'Half-past four.'

'OK. That's good,' she sighed, and walked away from us.

It was getting dark. We continued our search. Strange – remembering our little escapade after all these years, I don't recall it being dark. I remember it all in the white light of day. We searched house after house, reading their numbers aloud. At one of the villas, the Captain lingered, then called to me: 'I've got it,' he said. He pointed to a bell that said 'Alena Novotná.'

'Hey, excellent! Let's ring the bell!' I almost shouted. At that very moment I saw Mr. Kolman sliding down the bell-post. Almost discreetly. As if he didn't want me to notice. I caught him, lifted him up, and leaned him against the fence. He was light. He kept his eyes on me, silent.

'It's not here, I lied to you,' he said, breathing heavily.

'I'll call a cab,' I said, holding the Captain's fingers.

'No... Yes,' he sighed.

We stood there a moment longer, looking into each other's faces. Then I grabbed him around the waist, put his arm on my shoulders, and we went in search of a phone booth. But after just a few steps he stepped out of my grip and quietly told me he was fine and would walk on his own, which he did.

Darkness fell – I can see it now even in memory. The poorly lit streets of Břevnov, lights in the old windows, and the black conifers – back in those days they didn't have fairy lights – in the gardens. Just as I spotted a telephone booth and was repeating to myself what I would say about our journey back at the home, Mr. Kolman stopped in front of a terraced house and, with his eyes fixed on the facade, without examining the bells and the number, said again: 'I've got it.'

There was only one bell, and no name, but I didn't want to ring it. In my mind, I was already halfway back to the home in the taxi. I rang the bell.

In an instant, perhaps even before the sound of the bell had died away, the door opened and a young woman appeared in the yellow light. She stood on tiptoe to see beyond the gate, beamed, and called out:

'Oh, Captain! Come in. Mother and Grandmother are waiting for you. Where were you last year?'

A Summer Night

Michal Ajvaz

Translated by Andrew Oakland

I WAS APPROACHING ST. VITUS Cathedral from the Old Castle Stairs. Night had fallen, and the first stars were appearing in a clear sky. The chancel – a black silhouette of columns, flying buttresses and pinnacles – rose before me. The castle's courtyard opened up to my left. The place was deserted and so quiet, I could hear the water falling in its gentle arc from the mouth of the fountain's metal monster into its shallow basin.

I headed for the dark opening of a lane called Vikářská that winds along the right-hand side of the cathedral. As I stepped into the cathedral's shadow, from the impenetrable darkness behind a column, something jumped out at me. I caught a glimpse of a bulky and rather squat mass and heard a thump, as if a hard, inanimate object had landed on the cobbles. What followed was a sound like the sharp snapping of jaws which sent a chill down my spine, and I inadvertently let out a cry. The fabric of my trousers was gripped at the knee, caught in something's terrible maw. Instinctively I pulled my leg free and jumped to the side. Peering into the darkness of the lane, I tried to make out what kind of creature had leapt out at me.

There, on the cobblestones was a clam about eight feet long, still gently rocking on the curve of its lower valve from the impact of its fall. Now it was cautiously opening again. I do not believe that clams have eyes, but this one gave the appearance of watching me through its slit. A brawny leg slid out over the edge of the lower valve, touched the pavement, and with it the creature pulled towards me slightly. Then the leg retracted, but the shell remained open, as though the creature were waiting for something. It occurred to me to lure the clam to my home, where I would place a billiard ball inside it, feed it and wait for the ball to be coated with mother-of-pearl. In my studio flat, life with a clam longer than I was tall, and an undomesticated one at that, would be far from pleasant. But if it were to present me with the largest pearl in the world, wouldn't a few weeks of discomfort be a price worth paying? Besides, perhaps the clam could be tamed. I pulled a bread roll from my pocket, crouched down, and carefully held out my hand to the clam. It clattered its valves so menacingly that I retreated a few yards. A low growl may have come from the half-open mouth, or the clam may have been silent. On some nearby scaffolding I saw a long, thin strip of wood. I fetched this and eased it into the clam's black slit. In a flash, the wood snapped under pressure from the sharp edges of the valves – the kind of crunch a crocodile would've been proud of. The clam then opened and spat out the remains, before thrusting out the leg again and inching towards me. The edges of the valves were trembling, as though with a dark rage long nurtured on the sea floor. I quickly forgot the pearl the size of an ostrich egg.

The clam was now lying across Vikářská, making the lane impassable. If I were to try to slip around it, I knew it would snap at me again, and this time I might not be so lucky. I imagined one of my arms or legs being caught and then snapped between the valves, like that strip of wood. I turned my back on the thing and set off across the castle courtyard.

I'd only taken a few steps when I started to hear steady shuffling sounds behind me. Turning to look, I could see it inching towards me with its sub-aquatic gait, a movement that involved extending the leg, establishing a grip on the cobbles and pushing off. I needn't have been alarmed: although the clam seemed to be investing all its strength in the crawl, it was very slow. I took my time crossing the deserted courtyard, the wall of the cathedral high and sheer to my right. All the while I was aware of the monotonous, stubborn shuffle on the stones behind me. The next time I looked back I was about to enter the passageway. Light from the lamps along the wall of the palace was reflected on the smooth granite at the centre of the yard, as if on the cold surface of a lake; there, a black, oval silhouette lay still. The clam was resting after its exertions, the leg dangling over the edge of the lower valve like the tongue of an exhausted dog. I felt sorry for it. *I don't know what you have against me*, I thought. *Maybe I deserve your hatred. When we meet on the sea floor I will be at your mercy, but here in the city your exhausting efforts are in vain and causing you needless pain. How about you and I part in peace?* But once again the clam brought its leg down on the cold granite and resumed its slow and spiteful march. It was coming after me with such persistence one might have believed it had made the long journey from the bottom of the ocean for my sake only – to catch, chew on and devour me.

I arrived at Hradčany Square and descended to the stone balustrade, the lights of the city afloat below. I shall wait here for the clam to appear, I told myself. And moments later I did indeed see a sharp-angled black wedge appear in the castle gate beneath the statues of wrestling giants. The clam was edging its way out of the castle. Having moved out of the castle grounds, narrow end first, the clam stopped and used its leg to rotate. It must be looking for me, I thought. Perhaps it did have eyes inside its shell. Then again, perhaps it was sniffing the air for my scent, like a dog. It occurred to me that the clam really had stopped with its half-open visor pointed directly towards me. I couldn't shake the sense of being watched by a pair of small, evil, hidden eyes. Once more the clam set off purposefully in my direction. The square sloped downwards so the clam was able to slide, making its progress markedly quicker. Even so, it had no hope of catching me. I was getting tired of the whole thing. With a wave to the clam, I set off down Neruda Street, heading for Malostranské Square. My thoughts turned to other things. Before long, I had forgotten all about the clam.

But when I reached the arcade of the Smiřický Palace I heard once more the strange rattling and screeching, followed by a number of thuds. I turned back and froze: the clam was careering towards me down the steep street, bouncing off the cobbles, thrown from belly to back and back again, tossed from the one kerb to the other. Finally, with an ominous boom, it dashed against the closed gate in the portal of the Thun-Hohenstein Palace and a thin section of its shell chipped off from the edge. In the light of the streetlamp, I saw the gleam of mother-of-pearl through the break. I stood as if rooted to the spot, as rigid as the baroque statues on the palace facades. A group of Japanese tourists was emerging from the beerhouse U Kocoura. The clam flew between them like a cannonball, clipping a man in a raincoat who had been facing the other way, sending him flying backwards. Still, he managed to reach into his bag for a video camera and film the receding clam. Albeit in Japanese, his enthusiastic cries made me wonder if he considered giant clams to be a *Praga magica* attraction for foreign tourists, much like the Golem and executions in the Old Town Square.

When at last I gathered my wits, the clam was a few yards from me. I took off across the lower part of Malostranské

Square, weaving through parked cars, turning repeatedly to check on the horrifying progress of the mad creature. Behind the lit windows of cafés, the last customers of the day looked on with curiosity.

A lighted Number 12 tram arrived from the Klárov stop; I got on at the last carriage. As all the doors were closing and the tram jerked into motion, I heaved a sigh of relief. Standing at the back of the over-lit empty carriage, looking through the glass, I saw the clam fly across the lower square and strike the arcade of Malá Strana Town Hall with such force that it was tossed onto its back. There it lay pitifully opening and closing its valves as though gasping for breath. The tram turned onto Karmelitská.

I sat down on the rearmost seat and was overcome by a pleasant drowsiness. I would soon be at home under my duvet, I thought, and all the phantoms crawling in the city streets that night would be far away and of no concern. The shuddering carriage was lulling me towards sleep, and my eyelids were beginning to droop, when the tram came to an abrupt halt. Immediately I was unnerved. We were between stops, near the entrance to the Michna Palace. I rose from my seat to discover that workers were repairing the track in front of us. Impatient for the tram to start up again, I kept an anxious eye on the bend in the road beyond which Karmelitská meets Malostranské Square. The clam appeared sooner than I thought.

It was moving in fits and starts along the shiny track. Overcome by panic, I ran about the carriage and shook the closed doors, which refused to budge. The clam had achieved peak performance and was approaching the perfect crescendo. The smooth tracks made its progress easy. Again, the leg was extended, pushing the shell forward with machine-like regularity. It reached the back of the tram, placed its foot on the door and pushed itself upwards. Soon it was perpendicular to the ground, back up, thrusting the sharp end of its shell into the crack between the closed doors. I sat petrified on the seat nearest to them, watching the dark oval break in little by little through persistent, regular, jolts. Were these sounds the clam's snorts of exertion, or were they made by the rubber edging on the doors? I jumped up, gripped the clam with both hands and tried with all my might to push it out of the carriage. But my strength was meagre against the furious onslaught of the clam, whose blows against the doors were ever more powerful. It was as though the clam had transformed into a huge, unstoppable hammer. I sensed that it had given in to a dark ecstasy. Its thrusts came thicker and faster; there was triumph and jubilation in the thrashing of the doors. I knew that the doors would soon give way, and that the full weight of the clam would burst inside. As soon as the clam and I were alone in the carriage, my end would come, that much was clear to me. In all the years I'd been wandering about Prague lost in thoughts of phenomenology, surrealism, Hegel and Malá Strana dandyism, I'd often asked myself: where will all this end? I'd reckoned with all kinds of things – from terrible defeats to brilliant victories – but the possibility of being devoured by a clam on the night tram had never occurred to me. All manner of strange thoughts flooded my mind. I imagined the valves of the clam closing over me, leaving me lying in a dark, slimy dampness, then hearing a deep voice saying:

'You wanted to live with me in your one-room apartment. Now we will be inseparable. We can chat whenever we want or have deep conversations about philosophy. You can rest in a bed softer than those princes sleep in. I will give you pearls to play with. I will describe all the landscapes we travel through. In your benevolent darkness, you will see them in your mind's eye, in images more beautiful than the reality. You will never be troubled by snow or rain or a disagreeable wind…'

'No, no, you're very kind, my dear clam,' I'd reply. 'And I'm grateful for the offer, but wind and snow are no trouble to me, you see I'm used to them. I have business to attend to here, so I'd prefer to stay outside.'

'How ungrateful and impudent you are! If this is how matters stand, I will bite off your head, keep it and cover it slowly with mother-of-pearl, so making a masterpiece, the largest, most magnificent pearl in the world…'

At this point, the clam was two-thirds into the carriage. By the time the tram jerked back into motion, I had given up my futile pushing and was sitting resigned by the door. The clam was sticking out like a huge extendable indicator. It swayed helplessly for a while before falling away just as the tram was overtaken by a taxi. The taxi slammed into the clam and tossed it onto the pavement, where it upset several dustbins, which then clattered across the cobbles, spilling empty bottles, crumpled cardboard boxes and rotten apples as they went.

On reaching home I went straight to bed, where I fell asleep immediately. A few days later, I encountered the clam once more. A friend and I were driving along the motorway when I saw the clam dragging itself wearily along the inside lane. It was heading away from Prague. Could it be returning to the ocean after the failure of its mission? Might they now send someone else? Could it be that next time I'm chased through the city at night, my pursuer will be a squid?

My Libeň

Bohumil Hrabal

Translated by Paul Wilson

THAT LIBEŇ, THE OLD LIBEŇ, became my lifeline. I had realized, one day, that I could no longer go on living as I was. I'd become helplessly paralysed, unable to move either forward or backward, so I bade farewell to the Nymburk brewery and the little town in which my time had come to a standstill. I walked away from my beautiful four-room flat, then went through several sublets in Prague, even living in a steelworkers' barracks in Kladno for a while, until one day my cousin Milada told me that in Libeň, in a little street called The Embankment, there was a vacant room, a former ironworker's shop just off a courtyard that the owner was willing to rent to me for 50 crowns a month. And so it was that one day, at the beginning of the nineteen-fifties, I stood in this empty room, the air stuffy and smelling of mould, with a retractable lamp hanging from the ceiling, and I knew at once that this was what I'd been waiting for, that I was like a painter facing a freshly stretched canvas, and that from now on, what I would make of this room was entirely up to me. I bought an old art nouveau bedstead made of brass, a cast iron stove, and a table and several chairs. The landlady loaned me a sideboard, I spread a tablecloth on the table, a dazzling white piece of material, and set a bouquet of flowers on it.

I continued to commute to the Poldi Steelworks in Kladno, and I couldn't wait until my shift was done and I'd be standing once more in the middle of my own room. When I lit a fire in the iron stove and it cast patches of light on the ceiling through cracks in its plates, when the white table, with an open book on it, shone beneath the retractable lamp, in such moments I couldn't believe my good fortune. But, above all, I was fascinated by Libeň itself. I'd go on forays to places I'd never been before: the little street called The Embankment; the main street; the laneways leading to the Jewish quarter; Bratrská Street; Na Žertvách, a right-of-way where trains drawn by steam engines would ply their way; Kotlaska, and especially Rokytka Creek. I was enthralled by it all. I would go on walks at night, never able to get enough of the poetry of this quarter on the outskirts of Prague, dominated by the large, spherical gasometer on Palmovka. Each evening I would go for a beer at a different pub and, whenever I walked into a taproom and then into the main lounge, I felt as though I'd been struck by lightning, so in love was I with this outlying quarter of Prague, framed by Maniny and the Vltava and its navigable waterway, with the heights of Bulovka and Hájek and Červená Báň rising above it.

At that time, I had a feeling, which became a conviction, that all those laneways and streets, all those pubs, all of it had been prepared exclusively for me, that this quarter on the outskirts of Prague had been waiting here just for me, that it existed for my eyes and my eyes alone. All the residents of Libeň seemed to be cut from the same cloth I was, like the citizens of my Nymburk. I made friends with them, and every day I would eat with them and drink from our endless reserves of beer, at Hausman's, or the Old Post Office, or I would go with a jug to fetch beer from Liška's or from the Libeň brewery, from Kroft's, or Klouček's; sometimes I would carry my jug all the way to Douda's and the Merkur, just so I could enjoy walking through the laneways with all their illuminated taprooms. Almost every evening, and sometimes quite late at night, I would quietly climb to the top of Hájek or Šlosberk, and from those vantage points, I would drink in the view of Libeň spread out below me, with the twinkling lights of downtown Prague on the horizon.

When I surveyed the faces of the other dwellers of these outskirts, it would astonish me that none of them seemed aware of the beauty that lay all around them. Sometimes I would set out along the Rokytka Creek and walk all the way to Hloubětín, and every step of the way I'd feel compelled to stop and take in the bank above the creek, or try to determine what objects lay beneath the turgid waters flowing by. Sometimes, I would walk to the Vysočany railway station and, from there, delight in the poetry of the train tracks and the factories towering in the background. At other times, I would stroll along the main street all the way up to Ferkl's Inn, where it took me a year to discover that it housed the smallest cinema in Prague, in a room slightly larger than two third-class rail carriages combined. I would go to every movie they showed and couldn't get enough of the smell of the miniature movie house's mouldy floor, regretting that the year I moved to Libeň, they'd shut down the summer cinema in the garden, where the audience could drink beer and even smoke during the movie. Nevertheless, I would stand out there, the white screen long-since stained and cracked by the rain, and in my mind's eye watch all the films I'd ever dreamed of watching. And so I wandered around Libeň, stood by the chateau above the Kolčavka where, in the last century, there had been a pleasure garden with vineyards. The philosopher, Čupr, lived there, and in the Kolčavka, as the Rokytka was called then, there used to be trout.

At that time, I would climb over the fence by Libeň railway station and, in daylight or at night, I would walk through the old Jewish cemetery, sit down on one of the toppled gravestones and, sheltered under the lush foliage of an elderberry bush, be astonished again and again at how it seemed that everything had been prepared just for me, as though I and I alone had the eyes to appreciate all this beauty.

All at once, I had so many friends in Libeň that, in summer, I'd leave my window and door open so that everyone who was fond of me could come into my room, a place as public as a pub, like that dive bar, Na Dědince. I got married in that room, and I knocked down a wall to add another room, so that my wife and I had two rooms, with a toilet in the courtyard and a bathroom in the laundry. But there were still occasions when I had no time to make notes on my typewriter, I had so many friends at the time who'd just drop in unannounced, and sometimes an extra five or six people would sleep over. Yet I was happy, and I felt that I was writing a great novel with my life, that just as people would come and anoint me with their stories, so I would anoint them with myself. At the time, in the fifties, Vladimír Boudník lived in the next room and he too was in love with the outskirts of Prague. He loved, as I did, all the bizarre things about Libeň, and, like me, he didn't really need a studio. His small hand-operated press was enough for him; he could push his lithographs through that to create works that achieved a damnable level of charm and explosiveness, that had the power to wound. Every day, Vladimír and I would take the bus together to the Poldi steelworks, yet we were able to stay up all night talking and walking through old Libeň. Our first stop might be The Green Tree, then The Old Keg, and finally The Charles the Fourth, a pub Vladimír loved and where we had once felt honoured when, on the day before Christmas Eve, the publican closed the place early and brought out a harmonium along with his daughter and Mr. Vic – that was the publican's name – played while the regulars sang carols.

It was Vladimír who taught me not to mourn things that were being torn down, that were passing away. On the contrary, Vladimír loved taking me to where bulldozers were razing the walls of old buildings and entire blocks. It was Vladimír who taught me to love all that demolition and destruction. Even today, I stand with delight in Libeň and see how everything old and worn out, everything that no longer belongs, is being cleared away. Even today I like going back to my little courtyard at Number 24, The Embankment. The courtyard is overgrown, my windows are broken and, when I look inside the place where I'd been happy for an entire quarter of a century, I see with satisfaction that the floor is warped, the walls damp and crumbling, that no one lives here anymore, nor could they. Yet someone is still living up there on the balcony. I see diapers flapping in the breeze and I hear someone pecking away on a typewriter and, judging by the rhythm, that someone is trying to cram this billion-faceted world onto a sheet of paper that has only a single dimension, just as the lines in a text are one-dimensional. Yes, someone here is typing away, just like me, madly rattling away on the machine, then stopping to think things over, before resuming that flow of writing full of errors, just as I too once wrote texts full of typos. And someone in the flat above me, where the Slavíček's once lived, is making an account of himself and everything that surrounds him; the diapers are flying, so there's an infant there too, and the writer probably doesn't have an easy time of it either because the most beautiful thing about writing is that no one is forcing you to write, and when there's a reason to write neither a wife nor a baby is an impediment. I walk out under the fanlight of my former flat, the little courtyard is overgrown with shrubs. I open the door to the laundry and the Swedish washing machine is still there, along with the tubs in which we took our baths. The long workshop is gone, its walls collapsing and covered with filth, the roof where I once took a chair whose legs I cut short so I could put my typewriter on it and write my texts in the sun, is off kilter. From the neighbouring property a high wall rises from which chunks of plaster would break loose in the autumn rains and drop with a tremendous clatter on the roof of the workshop where they made paint and varnish. I walk down the stairs, and yes, that courtyard still looks like the deck of an old schooner. I walk through the corridor that is still as damp as it was when I lived here. I stagger slightly under the weight of nostalgia and the plaster rubs off first on my right, then on my left sleeve; I emerge into the street and that old gas lamp is still standing by the door. Then I walk back to the main street, smiling, and, where Bratrská Street joined The Embankment, there used to be a tiny little square, and I would tell Vladimír, as a joke, that when I'm famous, they'll call it Bohumil Hrabal Square... But today a bulldozer is hard at work, gleefully knocking down the little houses and the workshops where they made funeral lamps, followed by a small building with windows that once gave onto my little square, and I'm happy to be here to bear witness, happy to enter into the heart of this demolition site that no one is paying any attention to and, with a certain perverse pleasure, I can savour the moment of the old Libeň's sweet apocalyptic demise, my memories providing the key to the beauty I once lived by, and will go on living by until I'm buried by time, just like the Jewish cemetery and the workshop roof where once I wrote my texts in the sun...

All's Well in the End

Irena Dousková

Translated by Melvyn Clarke

ZEB HAD THOUGHT HIS mother would live longer. Maybe even into her nineties. That was the hunch he had about her — she had all the makings. As she grew older she dried up so much she was almost slim, and since she'd turned 60, when her gall bladder was removed, she'd practically not ailed at all. Her stiff knees bothered her, but that was all. She occasionally mentioned her high blood pressure, but everyone has that at her age, and it didn't show up in any way. She'd been widowed twelve years previously, and had been on her own ever since. She obviously missed Dad, a brooding biologist and loyal companion, but she had seemingly long since come to terms with it. She didn't seem to be suffering particularly from being on her own. If anything, she still didn't get much free time. Zeb assumed she'd be one of those indestructible grannies who stay marvellously lucid right to the end, and who have no time to die with all the running around they do. From the gallery to the library, from the pool to the cinema or the theatre. There were five or six pals, a whole bunch of professors, editors, translators and whatever else they used to be. They were all women – their menfolk had died or left. Only one, at least as far as he knew, was still married, and she kept the others supplied with stories about how Dr Kučera was slowly fading.

Zeb visited his mother regularly – they had agreed on Wednesdays and more or less stuck to them. If it didn't suit either of them, they chose another day or just skipped a week. No big deal about that. They were both quite rational, thank God, and could work things out together. She got along worse with her younger son Dan, which he knew was one of the few things that upset her. But it wasn't just his brother's fault – she had her share of the blame too. Every gathering, including all the holidays and family celebrations, ended in a row. She regretted it, but she still acted the same way the next time. She'd snipe at him, provoke him, and then grumble he had no sense of humour or detachment, and how awful that was. But the truth was he didn't have a sense for *her* humour, which was quite different after all. He hated his mother's caustic comments on political events or on her grandchildren's upbringing. In the latter case, Zeb didn't blame him; in the former, he did a little. He tried to persuade Dan not to react, since it was all pointless anyway. And he begged her time and again to leave his brother alone, or else not to complain that she only rarely saw him. Eventually he stopped though, as it was getting nowhere. They just couldn't help it.

She had no lack of humour or detachment, and Zeb must have inherited this from her. Joking was allowed about everything, not excluding Jews, of course. Nothing was sacred but the joke itself, providing it was a good one.

'He's trying to be funny,' she would say, leaning towards Zeb, whenever they came across some talentless wannabe.

She thought she was whispering. But she wasn't. As for the Jews, in recent years she had lost a little of her detachment. But she kept an eye on what was going on – she did keep some attachment.

'One hundred thousand! A hundred thousand Jews have decided to emigrate from France already,' she shouted. 'They murdered an old woman who survived the concentration camp. They threw her out of a window. And she's not the only one. It's happening again.'

'Don't be ridiculous. All we have here is Babiš, and he isn't going anywhere.'

'Leave it out, you know what I mean. It's all over Western Europe and it's coming here too – it's just a matter of time.'

'You shouldn't take it so personally.'

'So how should I take it then? Tell me. When Palestinians in Wuppertal throw Molotov cocktails into a synagogue and then by chance get caught, the German court calls it appropriate criticism of Israel. You know why? Because they're Muslims, like in France. So you're not allowed to say that. It's being swept under the carpet. All they talk about is right-wing anti-Semitism, Nazis and stuff. But that's just second division stuff these days.'

He didn't feel like talking about it. He knew she was pretty much right about a lot of things – he was keeping an eye out on what was going on too, though not with such masochistic obsession. But he wasn't going to encourage her.

'Do you want to come with us to the pictures on Saturday?'

'It's the lying that's the worst part. The cover-ups and the half-truths… They're just lies. They're just lying again. You can't sort out anything that you don't put a true name to first. But nobody wants to sort it out, certainly not the European Union. They're in charge.'

'Don't exaggerate…'

She was not going to be put off.

'If it was Catholics throwing the Molotov cocktails, then fine, it would've been talked about.'

'The Catholics have already done their bit.' As usual he let himself get sucked in.

'Just forget it – what have you got to do with it at all? What kind of Jew are you? They're not even after you. Don't go mad just because of one grandad…'

'That grandad ended up in Maly Trostenets concentration camp.'

'I know.'

'In what's now…'

'…Belarus, I know that too. We've talked about it loads of times. Look, I didn't mean to upset you. I'd take you right away if that's what you want, but I'm not a rabbi.'

He was going to say 'thankfully' but kept it to himself. How many of these uptight old women does a rabbi or a priest, same thing really, have to mollify every day?

'Everything has its rules, that's normal. I don't complain, I go to…' she pronounced the unpronounceable name of one of those associations where rejected adepts of Judaism meet, 'and I'm happy.'

He said he was glad, and they finally got down to eating. She had made borscht. When he complimented her on the soup, she laughed at how predictable he was. He probably was, but he really did like it. They played Scrabble. By then his mother was beaming with happiness. She won as always.

So now she was dead. It was all unexpected. It'll have been six months ago. He had kind of come to terms with it, but not yet taken it in. He had grasped it from without, but it had not yet quite sunk in. Particularly the finality of it. Somewhere at the back of his mind he kept expecting her to call. And make Wednesday Friday. No, not Friday. The Sabbath starts on Friday. That's when the Jewish association meets. Make it Monday. He also still had the round tin from Ikea in his cellar with Wintersaga written on it and his mother's ashes in it. Not that he was one of those penny-pinchers that we see more and more of every year, not at all. They'd held a normal funeral, family, friends, wreaths and so on. Except that he picked up the urn afterwards and then at home he poured the ashes into a Swedish gingerbread tin. He wanted to fulfil his mother's wish, as he'd once promised. Gingerbread wasn't actually part of that wish – but the tin was the best fit. He and Dan placed the empty urn in the grave next to their father. Dan had no idea it was empty – Zeb didn't tell him.

He hesitated for a moment, thinking that he'd tell him after all, but then he could just imagine his brother: 'Have you gone mad? The pair of you? You as well? I'm not surprised at her. No way, what bullshit!'

He quickly dismissed the idea. After all, unlike him, Dan hadn't promised her anything. It was purely his problem, he had to do it himself. It really was a problem, but he'd do it and be done with it. He'd just been waiting for the spring, and now it was here. But spring alone wasn't enough – it wasn't just to do with the ground loosening up a bit. This was the umpteenth winter in a row that it hadn't even had a chance to freeze over properly.

She wanted it to be at Pesach, so there were two weeks left. The most beautiful holiday, she was moved to say. She hated it when people called it the Jewish Easter. She said it was the other way round, but how was it the other way around? He didn't know what she meant – he hadn't listened to her properly. He didn't like it much anyway. He didn't do Christmas either – he just bought the presents.

'Do you know what Pesach is? The word, I mean, do you know what it means?'

He didn't. Unfortunately he'd forgotten again, even though she'd explained it to him a hundred times already. He was going to have to hear her out for the hundred and first time. He preferred trying to guess.

'Liberation? No, wait, freedom?'

'No, though it does have something to do with freedom. Pesach is naturally the holiday of freedom, but the word means something else. You seriously don't know? It means passing over.'

'Oh yeah, right.'

'Not just the Reed Sea, passing over has a lot of other meanings. Passing over the sea, passing over the desert...'

'Surely that lasted longer, didn't it? I wouldn't call forty years just passing over.'

'Over Pharaoh's will, over the Egyptian laws, and the angel passed over the houses marked with blood, and Moses over himself and his handicap...'

'And he killed someone too, didn't he?'

'He did and all – an overseer at a brickworks. He basically broke a lot of previously totally unbreakable dos and don'ts...'

'I get it, they passed over a bunch of unbreakable dos and don'ts so they could make up an even bigger bunch of unbreakable dos and don'ts. How many are there? Three hundred and sixty-five? More? Probably more...'

'Go to blazers.'

He could still hear her laughter.

She was happy with her would-be synagogue, particularly once she'd been through the conversion. He could quite understand; she wanted to prove to herself that she was serious. That it wasn't just some cheap flirtation with the esoteric by lonely women or women's magazines – she didn't like all that. Or rather she loathed all that, and she could get pretty militant about it. She really meant it. She had put a lot of time and effort into it, so that was fine by her. If it's worth anything, then it can't be for free. Until she was 47, she'd lived in a world where hardly anything could be taken seriously. She needed to believe in something, or needed at least to try. That probably involved the greatest effort. It was hard work, but it did work. She was 66 when she converted. A year after his father died. If nothing else, it got her through the worst of that. They washed the conversion down with Burgundy – kosher wine is too sweet. He congratulated his mother on finally being a full-cream Jew. Though she wasn't. For that she'd have to be Orthodox, which she could not be. Nor did she want to be.

'I'm not going to wear a skirt for the rest of my life,' she said, as if it were a veil.

'Course not,' he agreed, 'and one of those down to the ground and all. Crutches and knock-knees! At least we'll be spared all that.'

Everything was fine except for the grave. With her father's father as the only Jewish ancestor, conversion was not enough. Not unless it was an Orthodox conversion. As long as you're breathing, play as much as you want, with whoever you want and whatever you want, but forget the cemetery. She knew that well in advance, of course. She could only hope that something would finally change before she died. Though she wasn't that naive. She wouldn't have been able to live among those people for 30 post-revolutionary years. She didn't really blame them. The unorthodox society of which she was a member produced such a variety of exotics that she dreaded the idea of them presenting themselves as Jews anywhere else. The question remained if it would have been any different with the Orthodox Jews. It was actually not so much a religious problem as a social one. The collective is always a cock-up, but not belonging anywhere is an even bigger cock-up. She'd known that all along. The whole thing would have been funny, but time was running out. What about the funeral? What about the grave? Was she just going to end up in Olšany cemetery and confirm that life did not go on after her husband's death? That nothing else happened? That it was just a game? She loved games, but she didn't like this one. It was unwinnable. She decided to knock the pieces off the table.

If she couldn't get a place in the Jewish cemetery by legal means, she'd get there by other means. She picked out the one beneath Žižkov Tower. The one that was now less than a third in size because of the tower. She often used to take a walk there – it was a short way away. The second oldest cemetery in Prague, no burials had been allowed there for a long time. But that didn't matter – she'd have been an intruder in any other. She even picked out a specific spot, showed it to him one Wednesday and explained what he needed to do. Dig a hole, not too deep, just a little one, and put the ashes in. Preferably in a tin – urns are ugly and unnecessarily large. If things somehow got awkward, he could just empty it anywhere in the cemetery, she added, seeing the horrified look on his face. But she'd rather he buried her nicely in the earth. He didn't actually protest at first. Sure, he'd fix it up to her total satisfaction. He'd visit her and bring her flowers. Or stones if she preferred.

'You'll be close by – that's good, isn't it? You just have to climb the hill, but that's not a bad thing either – you'll be doing something for your health.'

'Thanks for thinking of me.'

'You're welcome.'

He thought it was all a joke. But she came back to it after dinner. And many more times after that. So he understood she was being serious. She wanted him to promise her.

'It would be totally against all regulations. The cremation alone. You get cremated and you're a goner. They won't even invite you to the Final Judgment.'

'It's been different ever since the Germans cremated six million Jews. Progressive Judaism recognises cremation.'

'Maybe, but the local community doesn't recognise progressive Judaism.'

'Well exactly, and that is why we have to do it in secret.'

'Your paper says that from next year you can get yourself buried in Brandejs. They're reserving a bit of space for the semi-skimmed and skimmed there. They still have to separate it properly, so that those who are already in there don't get offended, as some guy says in the interview. If you can hold on till the New Year then you might find space in Brandejs!

You mustn't pop your clogs before January.'

'I've never been to Brandejs in my life. What would I do there?'

'I don't know – what do people normally do when they're dead?'

As always, she stood her ground, as did he, as he tried to talk her out of the idea.

'I'd knock it on the head. I wouldn't gatecrash some place they don't want me in. You've never done it while you're alive – why start when you're not? You don't know what you're getting yourself into. Nasty neighbours will ruin your eternity. I wouldn't risk it. And what about Dad? He'll be disappointed…'

'Him? Please… He was only ever interested in fruit flies. If I'd moved to the far end of the country, he wouldn't have noticed.' So eventually he promised.

He bought a beer from the outdoors window at the corner pub and sat down with it on a bench. He wasn't alone – all the benches had someone sitting on them. Even though it probably wasn't allowed. He'd slightly lost track of what was allowed and what wasn't. Apparently no one here was bothered, just a couple of elderly dog walkers looked askance at the drinkers' exposed faces. Quite a few of them were walking here. Prague was almost deserted because of the virus, but the circular Škroupa Square was alive with the usual Žižkov life. After several cold days in a row, a warm April evening had arrived and had to be taken advantage of. Everything else would be fine. Not even the trees held back. The cold spring hadn't prevented them from spreading wide their crowns of fresh leaves, creating a fragile bower all around. They were all maple trees, branches covered in sprays of green blossom that every now and then tickled Zeb's head. He sat nervously, peering into his backpack, shifting it from side to side. In addition to the Wintersaga, it contained a small hand hoe. He had wrapped the two metal objects in newspaper so they wouldn't clink together and attract unnecessary attention. Over Mahler Park the clouds darkened, piling up like duvets that the tower might fall into with relief at any unguarded moment. He had another beer, as he waited for it to get completely dark. When it did, he started out for the cemetery. He'd walked round the fence again an hour previously, so he could get his bearings in the dark.

On a brick base there was a wrought iron grill fence made up of a series of iron bars that looked like large hammered nails. The fence wasn't high, but a steep slope lay in wait just beyond. If he hadn't known this, he would have climbed over and leapt sprawling into the ditch. Only along the final third was there an adjacent grassy stretch, but there the grill changed shape. The bars were set the other way round, bristling menacingly. Fortunately, the brick base was divided into columns. He had to climb over one of these – there was nothing else for it. He'd decided in advance which one it would be, and now he made his way towards it. Only there were still lots of people sitting on the wall and the surrounding benches with plastic cups in their hands. He definitely didn't need company. He turned and walked slowly back. It was no good – not yet anyway. But he wasn't going to give up either. He should have given up on the date, though. What would have happened if he'd buried his mother on Purim instead of Pesach? Nothing at all. Purim was two months ago. At that time the soil was already soft and there wasn't a soul on the streets. But it was too late for that now. He could wander around from Monday to Friday, week in week out, and it'd be the same. They wouldn't go back inside, not now. Not until next winter. They're hungry, they want a warm word of human kindness, they want booze, and as the guy wrote in that thread under some article, they don't just want to sleep with their own wives anymore. In that respect Žižkov Cemetery was probably going to be extremely unsuitable long-term. So what to do?

Maybe another beer, what else? He didn't expect a miracle, but he had some hope in those twenty minutes. It was really cold, and getting colder by the second. He didn't want to go to the park pub now, so he headed for U Mariánského Obrazu. Because of the cold, he bought vodka as well as Pilsner. Then he went back to the park. He grabbed a spot right next to the fence, but otherwise nothing had changed. They all had stamina, and perhaps there were even more of them now. The wicked spring up like grass, as the psalmist said. With the next batch he moved to a vacant bench – it was a little further away, but he had a good view. He was beginning to feel a little odd, skulking around like this all the time, though it was clear that no one was watching him. And that no one was bothered. Not even he was, as it turned out.

When he woke up, he could no longer see anyone there. He didn't know when everyone had left. He didn't have the strength to look, let alone climb fences. He was glad enough he managed to get up without throwing up. He slowly walked down to Kostnické Square. He didn't dream of his mother. For the rest of the night he didn't dream of anything at all, or did not remember anything. Then in the morning, after coming back from the toilet, a knot of snakes appeared to him. They were hiding in his laundry, slithery and slimy. He reached right in among them, and in a flash they had wrapped themselves around his arms and were moving up towards his neck. He was up at seven. Over coffee, which was the only thing he was able to ingest, he wondered if they could symbolise sidecurls. His wife wasn't talking to him, but she was surprisingly quick to respond to his request for help interpreting the dream. She saw his vices in the snakes. Ten minutes later, she also mentioned his fear of marital sex. Just at the door on the way out, she found another moment to explain that snakes aren't slimy. Not really.

He got into the second tram carriage. The number nine was half-empty – the crisis had its upside. He didn't sit down,

69

but stood on the back platform. It was nice to have it all to himself. He could have walked the few stations, but he wanted to clear up the cemetery thing in peace. He did try, but everything inside him rebelled against it. It wouldn't work. It just wouldn't. She didn't have to send snakes after him like that right away. She wasn't going to get anything out of it, and it wasn't funny either. It was all nonsense.

For years his mother had an article on her bulletin board cut out of some Jewish paper. She had framed it in black, underlined it in places, and put exclamation marks in the text. An Orthodox rabbi was responding to the complaints of his semi-skimmed fellows. He explained once and for all that he could not solve their family problems for them. If their fathers or grandfathers slept with blond Czech women and weren't bothered about following the law, then they were the ones to deal with. 'Do it,' he had urged his mother. 'You can do it now. He's right, that rabbi – I quite agree with him. Let's not make these transgressions worse after all. You can see for yourself the trouble it causes. Please don't ask me to do this. The ashes are going next to father and that's that. The family's supposed to stick together. He got off at Ohrada, glad there was no response.'

That night he dreamt he had a head full of worms. There were hundreds of them, writhing in his poor, greying hair and falling in handfuls on his shoulders. He didn't even have to ask what it meant. But he did, just to make his wife happy. For the sake of domestic peace, so to speak. 'Worms? That's obvious betrayal,' she responded almost straight away.

He parked in the square without any problems. It was almost empty early Saturday morning. Except for the Vietnamese, no one had opened yet. He noticed a Chinese restaurant and a pizzeria – they didn't look too inviting, but then he wouldn't have more than coffee anyway. He headed towards Schwarzenberg Castle, turned left just before it, crossed the

Blanice River, then left again – he didn't even have to follow the signs. He remembered the way very well – five years previously they had spent a week in a rented cottage nearby. His mother came to visit them, she liked it a lot. He walked down past a terrace of little houses, unostentatious, but nice in a pre-war way. He liked them like that. Strips of garden ran back from them, hidden from the eyes of passers-by, with apple trees everywhere, chickens here and there – the countryside, no more no less. Further on it was no longer quite like that. Here at the edge of the little town, the tacky houses had proliferated; the bigger, the uglier. At the expense of the apple trees, there was now more sumac and thuja. He left the local smart set behind and passed a car workshop and a warehouse. To the right the forest began almost without transition – after the last buildings came the first spruces. From the left came the smell of an unmown meadow, which could not get any more colourful than that even in summer. Daisies, hawkweed, poppies... If he had his wife here, she'd surely be picking a bunch. In his mind's eye he could see her leaping over the ditch and running in the grass. He smiled, though he was still glad to be on his own. The road headed uphill and soon the forest closed in on him on both sides. The undergrowth held in the moisture, and he could smell something else besides pine needles – a bitter smell, perhaps earth and leaf mould, maybe even mushrooms now. He heard a jay which had noticed him, though he hadn't spotted it. There was still a kilometre uphill to go before he got there.

Someone, he didn't know if it was Cohen, Haimie or Moses himself, asks the Lord: 'Here, could you not just choose someone else for a bit?' Now Mother *had* chosen him. She didn't dare ask Dan. Fortunately, that all ends today.

The gateway, or what was left of it, was just a rather large hole. In many places the brickwork had caved in, so all that distinguished the entrance from the other gaps was its central position and the ruins of the old mortuary through which it led. He walked in and looked around. The cemetery looked the same as it had five years previously. There was just more debris and self-seeding trees, while on the other hand there were fewer gravestones than he remembered. Not that they had decreased in number – it was just that he'd retained an inaccurate image in his memory. The reality was all the sadder. Then again the trees peering intimately close over the wall, their rustling and the birds singing in the otherwise absolute silence – all of that rang true. It was a romantic spot. At least so long as you didn't want to worry about the context.

Most of the gravestones, no more than twenty in all, were in the upper-left-hand section. Some were lying in the grass, others leaned over in such a way that they would clearly soon follow. A few were still standing upright. The impression of antiquity was in a sense false, caused by general neglect. Nothing here was older than the last decade of the nineteenth century, when the cemetery was established.

He chose a spot for his mother on the right-hand side at the top, almost in the corner. It wasn't next door to anyone or anything. There was just grass all round, with the dew still clinging to it, and behind the wall a huge spruce tree that would provide fine shade. He only hoped it wouldn't get eaten by bark beetle. He took off his backpack and got to work. It was easy – the heavy rains of the past few weeks had softened the earth. Within a quarter of an hour he had a deep enough hole, he put the tin into it, and packed the soil over and around it. On top of that, he placed the sods he'd set aside. You couldn't even tell he'd been doing anything. He cleaned up his small hoe, took out the stones he'd picked up along the way and made a circle out of them. At length he took several photos of the work, in case he ever decided to tell anyone in his family where to find his mother. He was relieved. It wasn't exactly what she wanted him to do, but it looked great. Hopefully they won't chew her out here. There were just a few of them, and they probably weren't Orthodox. Besides, he had put her in what was guaranteed to be the liberal section, which he had just established by this very act. He stepped back to take another look at everything from a greater distance.

'Guinea pig?'

He dropped his mobile phone with a start. There was a girl sitting on the wall. She was looking right at him. Who knows how long she'd been there.

'No…' he began, 'I'm…'

'I buried a budgie here,' she said, 'but that was a long time ago. I have a new one now. They won't let me have anything else. I'd rather have a guinea pig though.'

She might have been twelve, but she could easily have been fifteen too. She was Vietnamese and tiny – he couldn't guess. More like twelve.

'I didn't even have budgies. Only fish, but that didn't turn out well. One time we went off to the mountains, and when we got back, there was just this big ice cube in the aquarium. My brother had set the heater wrong.'

'That's awful.'

'It is. I wasn't that crazy about them, but it was awful. Totally Birds Eyed.'

She laughed, but got right back on topic.

'So what did you bury in there? What animal?'

'None,' he didn't know how to go on.

'What then? Money? If it was treasure you're going to have to bury it somewhere else, cos I saw it.'

He decided to tell her the truth. That was the simplest.

'It wasn't treasure. I buried my mother. Just her ashes of course. Because…' It wasn't that simple after all, 'she wanted to be buried in a Jewish cemetery and this is a Jewish cemetery. It was no good anywhere else. It isn't actually allowed. Not this way – just like that wherever you please. It's complicated. I don't know how to explain it to you in a simple way. I don't understand it all properly myself. It must be different for the Vietnamese.'

'I'm Chinese.'

He checked the time and blew the grass from off his mobile phone.

'Does that bother you?' she asked, as he didn't say anything.

'What?'

'That I'm Chinese.'

'No, why? I just couldn't tell.'

'Some people are bothered by it.'

'Some people are bothered by everything.'

'And you?'

'What about me?'

'What are you?'

'Czech, what else?'

'And your mother wasn't?'

More like fifteen, he thought.

'Sure, she was. Jews are Czechs too, more or less... That is, it depends. As I said, it's complicated.'

'That's what they always say about everything.'

'It's like you have it with the Chinese. Some are Communists, so no religion, others are Taoists, Buddhists... Some Christians live in China too. And Muslims. The comrades don't get on very well with either, but that's beside the point now. So, sort of. There are Jews here, but just a few. Fewer than Buddhists, I'd say.'

'Then again, there's an awful lot of Chinese.'

'It's better that way. There can be some hope that way, if you follow me.'

'I think so. Can I put flowers on your mother's grave? I often come here.'

'Sure, that'd be good of you. They'll survive it.'

'Who?'

'The dead. That was an attempt at a joke. We're supposed to put stones on Jewish graves rather than flowers.'

'I don't understand jokes much.'

'I have to go. What's your name?'

'Marie.'

'Really? That's unusual.'

'Well, we're actually Christians. My folks, that is. I don't think I really care.'

'Aha, my name is Zeb. Zebulun, to be precise, unfortunately.'

'That's unusual as well. Do you know anyone else called that? I don't.'

'I don't either. Bye then and thanks! Flowers will be fine.'

'Bye, nice to meet you.'

He gently touched his mother's grave by way of farewell. He hoped she'd enjoyed herself.

In the gap that used to be the entrance to the House of Life, he turned once more. The girl was sitting on the wall again. He waved to her.

'So why,' she called out to him, 'why is that your name, do you know?'

'Because my father was only ever interested in fruit flies,' he replied.

He had no doubt that in time she'd figure it out.

Realities

Marek Šindelka

Translated by Graeme & Suzanne Dibble

THE DRIVER SWITCHED OFF the radio. Dawn was breaking, the woman was sleeping and I could see her pupils moving beneath her eyelids. We drove around the city aimlessly for a bit longer until I ran out of money. The driver – a real salt-of-the-earth type – drove us free of charge for a while before finally stopping. I gently woke the woman and we stepped out into the sharp morning air somewhere in the outskirts. A gap in the clouds on the horizon, birds squawking, newspaper pages stuck to the railings, a plastic cup rolling around on the tarmac making a horrible plasticky noise. The door slammed shut and the taxi driver gave us an avuncular smile and was gone. It was getting light. We walked across a long, wide bridge high above a valley. A metro line passes through the middle of the bridge – we could feel it through our feet from time to time – and a four-lane road runs over the top of it, but just then it was empty. The row of round orange lamps stretching from one end to the other went out. In the depths below us were the roofs of houses, children in their rooms, mothers dreaming unsettling dreams full of equations, calculating the weight of suicides hurtling headlong from the railings of the bridge like fanged creatures in ties with wildly staring eyes, through the roof tiles and rafters, straight into their beds and cradles. They wake up drenched in sweat, and somewhere in their maternal bowels a stomach ulcer begins to form from the constant stress of death circling and throbbing above Nusle like a migraine.

We walk for a long time. Railings seem to sprout from this bridge as if they were alive. In the past they were barely waist-high, but then in the dark 1990s, when there were no mobiles or internet and humanity was generally lacking in entertainment, it was during these early hours of the morning that drunk entrepreneurs and spotty young politicians would drive from bars straight to work in convertibles welded together from Trabants and Ladas, champagne bottles dangling out of the door, fingertips skimming over the tarmac as if over the surface of a river, louts with the last vestiges of cocaine fizzling out of their bloodstream, while the city was whirling around them like a tornado and all the traffic lights were wearily flashing orange and there were birds and plastic bags in the bushes just like there are today – these bloodthirsty traders, raging at the failings of the system, giddy with privatisation, petulant and bored as they hurried towards their next adventure, would stop in the middle of the empty bridge and, screaming and whooping, throw random passers-by – old ladies with handcarts, homeless people and postmen – over the railings and into the abyss, and then, in their last twitches of consciousness, would plant razorblades on the chutes in the children's playground, stick syringes into the seats at the tram terminus and with the first rays of sunlight would fall asleep on a park bench covered by a coat made from unborn seal pups, their crocodile shoes placed under the bench as if they were in their own living room.

The woman protests that I'm making it up and I have to

go to great lengths to swear I'm not and prove to her that it's all true and that if we were here at this time of day in '91 we'd soon find ourselves flying over the railings. But it doesn't matter, that time is long gone, consigned to the pages of the history textbooks they sell for twenty crowns in second-hand bookshops. Time is not controlled by the antiquated plus sign but by the terrifying crack of the whip of square numbers, time shrinks and contracts, hurtling headlong into infinity, there is more and more of it, it is faster and faster, it accumulates and multiplies in all the receptacles we have devised for it. There was a time when people would go and whisper stories into the hollows of trees and cracks in walls. Today, 24 hours of time is added to YouTube every minute, which means four years a day. That intangible creature grows and grows – it ate the cart with the horses and the farmer, it ate the farmer's wife along with the piglets, and it'll eat you too, ha-ha. Anyway, a long time ago we were sitting in a kind of patisserie with a view of the city coming to life, drinking coffee and nibbling still-warm cakes called little coffins topped with whipped cream.

'What's your name anyway?' I spluttered into the cream. For a while nothing had been happening, for a while I hadn't been thinking and that completely flummoxed me, which I suppose is why I asked, I can't explain it otherwise, and the woman said:

'Anna.'

'Nice name – at the beginning and at the end roses are probably the same,' I recited, and Anna blushed and lowered her gaze to the hollow in the little coffin, and I saw for the first time that she was beautiful, but just then my phone rang and it was my good friend the Estate Agent. 'Hello, Estate Agent,' I said. 'Fine,' I said. 'We'll come,' I said. 'Tell me about yourself,' I said to Anna.

'There's not much to tell,' she said modestly.

'Don't lie!' I banged my fist on the table so hard that the

china rattled and tears welled up in Anna's eyes and she burst out laughing.

I became quite indignant: the opposite is true, Anna, there's so much to tell! There's too much! Look at me, you're like YouTube, you're full of foreign things and memories, you're a receptacle of time, you silly thing, you're the detonator and the explosion, you're the thousand and one nights squared, you're evolution and creation, you're a node in the network, you're the network itself, you have over three hundred friends – not bad, you've never seen them in your life but you know them like the back of your hand, day and night they tirelessly write and tell you what they've just had to eat, what they've had to drink, what film they've seen that they stole off the net, what they think about the war in Mali or Georgia or in some other country that's been made up for the purposes of the TV news. You have a bank account where you hoard non-existent money that you use to pay off non-existent debts or buy machine-distressed jeans or travel to non-existent countries where you are moved by the sight of poverty through bullet-proof glass and the misty veils of your expensive vaccinations.

Don't be coy, Anna. There's a whole world, a whole universe within you, there is infinity in every millimetre of your skin – I kissed her on her infinity – Anna, my love, tell me about yourself, I'll write a book about you (Anna clutches the table top in fits of laughter, leaning back with tears rolling down her face), I swear to you, you won't believe it but I'm a writer, stories disgust me, there are too many of them and almost all of them are the same, but not yours – your story doesn't actually exist, your story is that you long for some kind of story, for romance, passion, you long to break free of your chains, but the problem is that there are no chains, romance is outdated and ridiculous, all stories are second-hand, distressed by a machine, and you don't want to shop in this brothel stinking of mothballs where convention runs rife like syphilis.

REALITIES

Anna, your eyes see it: passion hasn't existed for a long time, only the instructions for passion, sad tutorials that occasionally arouse us, sad videos where a bodybuilder rapes an anorexic girl according to a script. Erotic websites where grief is divided into twenty categories according to various practices so outdated they make you want to weep. And then when you meet someone, when you meet a man you could have something meaningful with, a man you like, then as soon as you undress it's as if a red light has gone on in Pavlov's laboratory, as if someone has snapped a clapperboard and shouted *Action!* You see how those frightened men, their brows beaded with sweat, try to fit into one of those twenty categories, how they caper about you and do their exercises according to the script, and finally when they are lying there, affectedly panting and pretending to feel the pleasure slowly fading away inside them, like frightened little boys they ask in a roundabout way if the performance was a success, if they were good in their role, and tears gather in the corners of your eyes. You are silent and the men withdraw into their shells and inwardly fondle themselves, comforting themselves and working themselves up for an even more hysterical acrobatic show, an even wilder display of abandon and passion.

Anna, what are we going to do together? I doubt I'd be any better, nor would you. Our century's love life is perhaps an even bleaker activity than tourism. Anna, my love, there's a deep frost within us. We could go over to my place right now, struggle into those ready-made costumes of male and female desire, check our depilation and observe how our movements are spoiled in advance by this wretched convention. There's nowhere left to go, the body has too few orifices and the number of positions is finite, there's nothing to break down, the rock 'n' roll of the body has long since faded out, the lead singers have been shot and there are too many revival bands to count. Anna, thirst is a poor synonym for passion, thirst is dry and desperately unerotic. We'd be thirsty together all night long. My friend, the Entertainer, was right when he said that, when all is said and done, sex is just exercise.

I looked out of the window: above the city, which was sunk down in a sort of chasm here, the Nusle chasm (Prague is one big valley), the clouds were breaking up and rolling away as the sun broke through them. From somewhere in the depths, in the distance, in the ruins of the Národní Třída metro station, as quiet as the ticking of a wristwatch or the clicking of a vault lock, came the sound of pneumatic drills. A pit from which something new would emerge with a screech, but for the moment it looked like a hip operation, a deep crater with all kinds of things in it that were probably better left unseen. That's how you break into a city: you place your stethoscope roughly in the vicinity of Letná Stadium and listen carefully to the clicking, trying to figure out the combination. However, this city, which expands around us like a bodybuilder who's overdone it with the steroids, which keeps being built up before falling apart again, doesn't seem to have a combination.

The night is long since over, Anna. I have another suggestion: let's go and see my friend the Estate Agent, there's a party going on at his place, it's getting light outside and the day is bound to be complicated. But first tell me something about yourself, or don't, let me guess: you're 31, you're frighteningly beautiful, your name's Anna, I see you sitting by the window of a café in a kind of timeless state at the start of a hot spring day, which might not even start because we're going to prolong yesterday for as long as we can stay on our feet. We journeyed through the night in a taxi – now, that definitely counts as something real! The windowpane reflects your image like a mirror, you look at yourself and you can clearly see all the little bumps and irregularities that show up on your face. You marvel at all the things a person has to lug around inside of themselves, so many foreign things they never asked for. Anna, you are a walking question mark. You are as enigmatic as a trailer for a Hollywood blockbuster. You are successful and profitable. You are perfect, the world around you is perfect, and that's the problem because you merge into the background and you start to long for a flaw in all of this, for some kind of defect.

Anna, I'd better stop talking, let's watch TV, the wretched pastry chef behind the counter with a physical dependence on sucrose has just switched on the box, though instead of a test card it is, of course, the Entertainer who appears – he's hardly been off the television lately, whimsical, positive, smiling, he got the better of his own heart attack just like Kate with the Devil, eyes like two light bulbs in which the tungsten wire glows red. 'A person can endure anything,' the Entertainer explains to the young presenter (who is perfect on the surface but otherwise, beneath the skin, cobbled together like Frankenstein, especially as far as her thoughts are concerned). 'Good morning,' she says as if she had discovered America. 'The best thing to do in the morning is go for a run or at least do ten squats,' this psychosomatic monster explains to the nation. Fortunately, the experienced Entertainer is there to take the helm: 'In Germany, overgrown catfish are on the rampage [laughter], they eat swans and behave like cannibals [the presenter laughs too as she tries to learn something], attacks by giant catfish are terrifying and deeply unpleasant [laughter, advert].'

I ordered more of the little coffins. 'Another thing they discovered is that all cyclists are into blood doping,' continues the Entertainer. 'Like a vampire – like the ouroboros – Lance Armstrong had his teeth sunk into himself for years, drinking his own blood, which is truly shocking, my friends – people are capable of unbelievable things,' says the Entertainer, shaking his head, 'but a good friend of mine who is in the real estate business once had a salutary thought: why not allow doping? Why not make it easier for all these tortured athletes? Sport is a celebration of the body, so why not celebrate it in style? Let's leave the boyish contests to the Scouts and feast our eyes on some real musculature. I'd love to see a marathon completed in ten minutes, a five-kilometre javelin throw. I'd enjoy watching some beefed-up Japanese and German flesh battling it out in the ring. Some hunk of brawn climbing up Mount Everest without oxygen or while holding his breath. You see, in spite of everything, mankind is inclined towards a certain growth – the greatest effort goes into creating barriers which are then broken down in an extremely convoluted way. There's one thing I've always said: the brain is a good shepherd, the secretary of the politburo, the party chair, the generalissimo. The body is the community, one knows how to do this and the other that, you know how it goes. But I ask you, why stand in the way of true self-fulfilment...'

The pastry chef changed the channel to 'Cooking with some actor or other', where someone was in the middle of making something horrendous. A doleful lethargy settled over the pastry chef's expression once more and he looked at us like an old metal welder stupefied from constantly breathing in aluminium.

We decided to leave. Anna, we have to be careful that a story doesn't develop between us. I've got experience of this kind of thing. Even an ordinary trip from a cake shop to an estate agent's party can spawn a ten-headed monster. And yet it all begins so insidiously. The story takes hold somewhere in the mysterious tracts of time and begins to grow. Right now we can play about with it, but it will begin to branch out, take root within us and transform into affection, memories, even love! And finally it will grab us by the throat and force us to remember, compare, reproach one another for some misdemeanour or other – it'll sink its teeth into us and drink our blood like Lance Armstrong or even worse.

Anna, I know all about stories. I've already told you I'm a writer (I have to wait a while for Anna to stop laughing, she doesn't believe a word of it). Seriously – at the age of fifteen

REALITIES

I wrote a 700-page historical novel called *Hitler's Sister* in the popular genre of 'the fate of an ordinary person against the backdrop of great historical events' (take the Second World War, add an ordinary person and alternate variously in a ratio of roughly 3:4 until a message emerges). A year later, to great acclaim, I published a romantic drama with a philosophical bent called *Love Behind the Iron Curtain* (the book essentially covers the same in 500 pages as the title does in five words. If you ever fancy trying it, the formula is as follows: communism, love, philosophical musings, all of which alternate in various ways in a ratio of approximately 3:4:1 until a message emerges). But at the age of seventeen, when I got to know life, I became embittered. Suddenly I realised that there was no longer much difference between the words Holocaust and Transformers. Both of them belong to a strange, distant universe. We desperately need stories, we can no longer live without them – like the pastry chef and his sucrose, I suppose, or the welder and his aluminium. It seems to us that our identity, our roots, our past, stare out from them. But it's all a lie, Anna, we don't see ourselves as we are. None of these stories offer an insight into the past – they offer an insight into Google. Reality doesn't have a story, only an infinite number of shards which form more and more new patterns in this mad kaleidoscope of our short lives.

In the end, all evil is transformed into a twisted romance. Into a product. Into a comically marketable commodity. Hitler is the true saviour of marketing. Call something Hitler and you've got it made. Anna, believe me: Hitler draws people's gazes like a pretty girl. Move Hitler from side to side and people will watch him like a tennis match. Every historical character becomes a brand, a pathetic symbol consisting of two or three Wikiquotes. Something tasty which can be consumed simply and quickly and is easy to digest. I became aware of this one particularly melancholic evening when all that autumnal swaying of branches and creaking of roots was going on across the city – I came home, parked my Picasso car, and because I was feeling down I drank a bottle of Napoleon cognac and then a half bottle of Amundsen vodka. All I could find in the fridge were some Mozart chocolate balls and a Charles IV camembert that was past its sell-by date, a half-eaten Rembrandt doughnut and a packet of Matisse cat food. With the last of my strength I crushed some ice in my Bosch mixer to make a Hemingway cocktail, and finally (because I really was at a low ebb) I downed a bottle of Dali aftershave, curled up on the couch and fell asleep to the crackling of my crappy old Tesla television set, worn out by the whole of Europe.

Anna, watch out!

The world's around us!

Look after it for me for a while. There's a light rain, the kind that turns the roads into mirrors that flip the city upside down. The clouds move along, occasionally revealing a patch of sunlight. We don't feel too bad after all. At a newspaper stand – where the Entertainer stares out like an owl from the front pages because he's cheated on someone again – I buy a half litre of rum and then we walk through the wet park, huge drops glistening on the leaves in the sunshine. We drink the rum, that amber in glass, that distillation of Christmas, that essence of praline, it tastes like childhood. Anna, close your eyes, on a deep winter's night as black as Malevich's square children hold their breath and the baby Jesus wanders around the house. No one has a clue about the powers of hell yet, except maybe Mum and Dad, they've experienced a thing or two, but the children are unspoiled, they dream dreams as sweet as rum.

Anna, wake up!

We can't sleep here, I say with a smile. The wood of the bench is black, softened by water, the grass squeaks, the sunshine is starting to heat up and steam is rising from the ground. I look at you, snoozing on my shoulder, bathed in the light of a new day. One day I'll write a book about the corner of your mouth, the tiny wrinkle that just flickered between your eyebrows. Anna, where did you come from? I was as used to my own life as the inside of my mouth, but ever since you showed up it's as though one of my teeth has been filled in.

Come on, then.

You squint into the sunlight and smile sleepily.

We walk through the city, all this stuff around us, look! I hold up the screen of my mobile and all the buildings start talking and offering me their products, the restaurants present their menus to me like enchanted waiters transformed into real estate, the taxi explains how much it will cost to take me to the airport. Sitting behind a wall I see a friend of mine – someone I've never seen before but have lots in common with – and he's giving a thumbs up to the Entertainer's morning show, which he is watching on his tablet while twittering away to his Uzbek friend on the other side of the planet. The world is so rich, Anna. We've coated it with another layer of reality which entertains us and makes us money. Now we just have to unlearn how to eat and breathe and a few other relics of the past and we'll be truly happy. It suits me down to the ground – I liked constructing things out of Lego when I was young and today you can construct your entire life. You can bet anything you like that your neighbour is living in a completely different universe to you. Incidentally, I recently found out that my neighbour is something like a grandmaster of overclocking CPUs. He's famous in his own way. His name's Míša, he's thirteen and he's completely translucent: when he stands facing the light, you can see purply-blue clusters of arteries and veins pulsing away in his ears and in his little forehead, troubled by all that processor alchemy.

Anna, sometimes I miss reality. Recently my friend the Estate Agent invited me to a party, a charming little soiree for 350 employees from the branches of his estate agency. He only takes on people between the ages of 18 and 25, no gerontobusiness, as soon as someone matures even slightly, they're out – they're impossible to work with, explained the Estate Agent before disappearing into the crowd for the rest of the evening. I sat at a table of barely adult IT experts who got completely plastered and only spoke in numerical codes, but eventually a kind of melancholy crept up on us, entering the boys like a ghost in the machine, and they began to get nostalgic. They remembered how five years ago they had stayed up all night playing a shoot 'em up on the web and all of a sudden, unhinged from the lack of sleep, they found themselves in a strange warehouse, a rusty, broken-down hangar or something, with burnt-out Messerschmitts, bits of old war machinery, half the roof torn off and a gentle rain falling inside, but the sky ragged, the way it sometimes is at dawn or dusk, with raw streaks of colour. Crackling on walkies talkies. There are five of them and they're in bad shape, one of them seriously wounded, all of them nearly out of ammo, and somewhere in the darkness amidst all this junk roams a cyborg: neither man nor machine, a huge monster, muscle attached to metal, wires and tubes in its arms, the body fuelled by kerosene or something, a red telescope instead of eyes and bazookas instead of hands. They don't dare to peek out much because if it spots them they're doomed. They can just hear those menacing footsteps, the hiss of hydraulic pistons. Occasionally it stops and they hear it zooming in with its eye like some kind of monstrous paparazzi, scanning the surrounding darkness. They daren't move, so they write messages to each other instead – someone is annoyed that they've wasted all their remote-detonated mines, and the cyborg, as though it has overheard, stops and listens – as though it was thinking. Not a peep out of anyone and then finally those thundering footsteps again, the pistons, tendons covered in metal. *I've got one grenade*, someone writes; *I've got two*, someone else says, *that's all*. They argue for a while. They're done for, the machine is too powerful. And at that moment the one who's seriously wounded pipes up, the one who's in the red, on fourteen percent health, the one they call Zilvar. *You draw him off with your fire, I'll run over there, hide behind a barrel and blow it up, give me the grenades.* No way! writes the leader quickly. But Zilvar is suddenly cool, determined, reconciled. There's a moment of silence filled with emotion. Then the ones with the grenades come over and empty them out of their equipment packs onto the ground in front of Zilvar, who picks them up. Then the leader himself comes up, so close he can make out the individual pixels of Zilvar's face. They stand facing one another without a word, but there is no keyboard shortcut for an embrace. Silence, the rain falling into the puddles around them, the terrible footsteps growing distant in the darkness. *Now!* someone says. A few rounds are fired into the dark. And Zilvar runs. He rushes to meet his fate, he is no longer aware of anything, he charges into the darkness, into the final battle, he thinks of nothing, he is pure – just hold on and destroy that cursed human being transformed into a machine!

They fall silent. We're at the Estate Agent's shindig, but it's as if the world around us has ceased to exist, as if it has lost its contours. I feel moved as I sit there with the boys. One of them, his eyes red, lifts up his drink and I clink glasses with them all. As if I had been there too, as if I had experienced something real with them, something to remember.

Anna, that was all a long time ago, so long ago that no one even knows anymore how far down in whichever digital realm that longing, that bitterness, has settled. I think of that one place it might be nice to return to, one little corner, to find my own Wailing Wall there, to go backwards through those spent rounds and levels, a pointless soldier heading in the wrong direction, nothing lurking anywhere, the seasons standing still. I'd like to walk around there, I'd find my wall and somewhere between two pixels I'd whisper into a digital bullet hole all the stories, all the things I don't want to live with.

Anna…

Anna?

Are you there?

You had me worried. What would I do without you now?!

Anna, look, over there! And here. *Flaws!* We walk through the city and look at the flaws, they're everywhere. Advertising hoardings full of bodies. We have witnessed the dawn of an era when the marketing strategists realised that no one gets excited about perfection anymore, no one notices it, sensorily overloaded consumers are much more attracted to defects. Instead of chiselled athletes and models, the billboards and TV and internet adverts began to be populated by freaks. Look at that! A woman whose face looks as if it has passed through the intestinal tract of a herbivore with at least five stomachs – tongue sticking out, nostrils flaring and eyebrows bristling, she's trying to tempt us to switch banks. The monster is saying a number to us; the interest rate is written in a bubble and there's an arrow pointing to the woman's mouth. And over there! A radio station has based the advert for its morning programme filled with laidback tunes and cheery presenters (Entertainer + extras) on the slogan *Exchange a Smile*, which it decided to illustrate literally in its campaign. This means that the city is now teeming with posters of wretched mutants, creatures from the photo album of a deranged plastic surgeon: the graphic designer has sliced through the head of a rancid old codger with liver spots spreading over his bald pate like continents on a globe and stuck the drooling gob of a laughing baby under the old man's nose. The baby was then given the bearded chin of some alpha male, while the top half of the alpha male's head stared helplessly above a girl's pouting red lips, the upper half of the girl's head morphed hideously into the old man's dried-up gums, and so the freakshow came full circle, or continued along in a spiral on other billboards and illuminated hoardings.

We walk through this forest of beasts, Anna is smiling and I can understand why, I have a weakness for monsters too. I find *the flaw* more appealing than the sci-fi families from the previous marketing era, manufactured according to a template: bodybuilder father, peroxide anorexic mother, two children who are mini versions of the parents, families from an incubator, grown out of saline solution on cotton wool, insufferably happy cultivars from some kind of parallel universe that consumers are forced to peer into through the window of billboards, TVs and mobile phone screens. It really had become impossible to look at that anymore, it made you want to destroy something rather than buy something – not quite the desired effect, muttered the strategists, rubbing their foreheads and shrugging their shoulders sheepishly at meetings. There followed many sleepless nights, muscle spasms and bloodshot eyes, the breakdown of old marketing friendships and marriages, the transfusion of young blood and then old blood too (you never know), several caffeine overdoses, dozens of disrupted biorhythms, a few burnouts and one spontaneous combustion before they finally came up with *the flaw*! With trembling hands they brought it forth, still wet, into the light of day and advertising started to become defective. The success was phenomenal. The strategists rubbed their hands, they saw that people couldn't resist defects – as soon as one of the creatures appeared in their peripheral vision they'd rush to examine it, shake their head at it, but along with the defect the name of the radio station or the bank, the barcode for biscuits or washing powder would be written into their nervous system and perhaps even into their DNA. Defects work like a magnet, Anna, people long for flaws. Everything is too safe, too clean.

The Entertainer was once on the radio entertaining humanity and explaining: we disinfect everything. We disinfect everything before we even injure ourselves. We wear clean clothes, gargle with mouthwash and shave off every hair on our bodies, we swallow vitamin C for our health and vitamin E for God knows what, calcium for our bones, folic acid for our blood, ginkgo biloba for wisdom, extract of green tea for immortality, and so on and then we go to the cinema to watch a family movie about the Holocaust or the extinction of 99% of the human race and the destruction of civilisation as we know it by some monster that emerges from the depths of space to devour it.

Anna, we both like going to see films about the destruction of the human race and similar amusements, we have so much in common, you are happy in this world, you understand its diversity. But not everyone is so eager to bathe in infinity. At one point during the programme *Cooking with the Entertainer*, the Entertainer asked a politician while mixing a sausage goulash: 'Why do you think people are so fond of war?' 'I don't know,' said the politician [sweaty brow, fingers behind his collar, a great cloud of steam rising up from the goulash], I can't say I've noticed they are fond of it [smile, sweat, moustache].' 'With all due respect,' said the Entertainer, 'you don't have a clue. People are fond of war because it's simple. Much simpler than peace. You have no idea how many people these days secretly long for totalitarianism, for something awful to happen, genocide, terrorism and the like. They're tired of this awful ambiguity, they're not built for it.' The Entertainer picks up a wooden spoon, narrows his eyes, blows, sips, he's not satisfied, the politician continues mixing strenuously [sweat, moustache, smile – then just moustache]. 'Our bodies are machines built for survival,' continues the Entertainer, putting his arm around the politician's shoulder in a chummy manner. 'We have huge reserves within us, our bodies are weapons, we are primed for battle, for adversity. Our physiology isn't prepared for the possibility of plenty, our brain becomes terribly bored: if it doesn't have totalitarianism it creates its own. The brain is a capitalist. It's an evil bourgeois that hoards time. It exploits the whole body for its own dark ends, it possesses all the means of production and reproduction, it can talk, it can deceive, it can work the rest of the organism to death in the name of an entirely abstract ideal. In the name of spiritual salvation, which the intestines and gallbladder couldn't care less about, it is capable of killing them off – and ultimately itself too. It forces poor yogis to hold their arm above their head for 30 years until it turns into a bony twig rotting alive, it forces anorexics to wither away and athletes to swell up like balloons, it poisons the whole body with alcohol in the name of pleasure, we wring the hormones out of our adrenal glands, it is a rampant wild animal coveting time and memories, which it frantically exchanges with other nervous systems. Ladies and gentlemen, the body is a political structure, a multicellular dictatorship. Cells are born and die obediently, with discipline, they work themselves into the ground and then die trampled upon by thousands of others. The heart – that crazy oscillator overclocked by God knows who and when, that rhythm that has been passed on by millions of mammals since time immemorial – the heart as a metronome to which the entire organism sings its bloody living and working song – not even Sebastian Bach himself ever played the kind of fugue we are performing here – the bodies of the higher primates are singing, the bodies of genus homo, learning to divide their limbs, bodily orifices and skin formations into the clean and unclean, the forbidden and the permitted, learning to hate their bodies and feel ashamed of them – mix it properly or it'll separate!' The politician, who was staring like a turnip the whole time, quickly jiggled the wooden spoon and said something to the effect of: 'Well, our primary concern is the family, and, if I can put it like this [moustache], a kind of basic decency, children...' and he began to spout a lot of nonsense until I was forced to switch off the TV and continue with my yoga or Tai Chi or holotropic breathing or whatever it was, I wasn't all that sure myself.

We walk through the city where even the advertising

strategists longed for a flaw and that longing began to earn them a tidy sum. Everyone longed for it. We stop for a moment in front of the six-foot codgers in an enormous backlit billboard who are grimacing, blushing, sticking out their tongues, baring their toothless gums and tearing out the last threads of their hair because they didn't get their supplementary pension sorted out in time. And as though we were standing in a birch grove, we kiss in this thicket of hideous pensioners. It's wonderful, it's a miracle, there have been more kisses in the world than there are stars in all the galaxies and yet here in this forest of old men it still feels like something new. Like a first. Perhaps all this deformity around us has highlighted the beautiful simplicity of another person's mouth. We have a bit of a fumble, I put my hand under Anna's skirt, we kiss under the scarlet codgers as though beneath a blossoming cherry tree. I think I'm in love, Anna. But Anna has slipped out of my grasp. Unfortunately we're not in a thicket but at a tram stop, we have to go, there's no time, the morning hell is about to break loose. The rain in the bushes will dry up just like our fragile, sleep-deprived nervous systems. We walk through the streets which are filling up with people, everyone chasing after their own heads in which awful things are taking place, things you don't want to know about for love nor money yet can't avoid. It's precisely at this time of day that I regularly begin to feel the pearl of a migraine in the middle of my forehead, white as a cooked fish eye. Anna, I suffered from terrible headaches before I met you, I was losing my vision because of them. The whole world got embedded within me and cut into the inside of my skull with a barb, because even I lug around that infinity within me, even I am full of foreign things I never asked for which occasionally group themselves into a form that hurts. But you came to me like a Samaritan, like an ice crystal, like the coolness that spreads over your tongue when you swallow a snowflake, you made all the pain go away. I can speak to you, I know that you hear me.

REALITIES

People are terribly alone, Anna. Not in the usual sense that people write about in poems or in the tabloids. They are alone with their own world, with their own superstructure which no one understands except them. They have no one to share it with. The birds on the roofs weave their nests in the tops of antennae and couldn't care less that the internet is running through them, that the Entertainer is passing through them with a gentle metallic tingling, like the kind you get when you lick a tap. They don't care that someone is downloading porn through their chicks, they are pure and free. Foxes have learned to live in rubbish bins, all sweaty from the glutamate, and howl at the moon with tongues lacerated on tin cans. The cow may have been transformed into a milking machine but it is completely unaware of this – it doesn't know it's nursing half the planet of great apes, who dream their conscious biodreams on the internet and watch their cow in the pasture through their webcam and make sure it's living the right way and grazing according to the manual they got at an animal rights demo.

Mankind is the only endangered species on this planet. He fears for his own world. Once that oversensitive shepherd known as homo sapiens quits the field, it will be a matter of total indifference to all those blissfully ignorant habitats, the forest definitely won't complain that there is no longer a higher primate marching about with a rifle, monitoring the condition of the game animals. All of these species will just gently shake off all the unnecessary names, terms, classifications and affiliations, and merge into one blissful unity – which in reality they have always been. We are alone, Anna, it gives off a chill wind. We've fired monkeys, dogs and even ourselves into space, we've sent coded Mozart and a scanned Mona Lisa by radio waves and – I could almost weep it's so poignant – we expect to find someone as lonely as us somewhere in the clusters of galaxies. This intergalactic mating call, this radiotelescopic courtship! We peer into the frozen black-on-

95

black abyss of the cosmos, we sing Mozart the way children sing to banish their fear of the dark. We show the Mona Lisa to the Milky Way the way we would show it to mummy or the teacher, expecting a reward, but the Milky Way just stares at the portrait impassively and indifferently. It's like showing a picture of an orangutan to a horse.

Incidentally, at the start of the century there was a horse which took pity on us and began to think – you can Google it. It began to count, multiply and divide. Its master, a retired maths teacher called Wilhelm von Osten, drilled it in its times tables, called it Clever Hans and began to make money from the horse. Around the same time – perhaps it didn't want to be outdone – a dog in Mannheim also began to think. It was called Rolf and it left behind a book of memoirs and extensive correspondence. It thought and spoke – with a Palatinate accent, no less – by slapping its paw. Towards the end of its life the dog settled down, became a poet, voracious reader and political commentator, learned several languages and, according to its owner who took it for walks, eventually became rather embittered and morose. It began to grapple with philosophy and theology, pondering the meaning of its own existence until the owner became ashamed of her own superficial interests. Anna, you're laughing, but I swear it's true. Der Kluge Hans – Clever Hans – came to a miserable end, became defective: a careless or vindictive groom (the horse was much better at counting than he was) brought a mare into the yard and the virgin Hans, who up until then had lived a strict monastic life of celibacy, science and the chaste intoxication of numbers, the exemplary Hans lost his head and out of sheer passion tore open his belly on the crossbar of his stall. They had to stuff his intestines back in and sew up his stomach. The supreme equine mathematician lived out his final years miserably in a green meadow near the town. Old Hans degenerated into a horse again. The wise dog grew bitter and silent and once more humanity found itself alone in the middle of the frozen infinite cosmos, out of whose depths the Big Bang winked at it mischievously.

That was all such a long time ago. For several hours we've been sitting on a couch at my friend the Estate Agent's place. A party has been going on for three days in one of his countless apartments. The Estate Agent trades in real estate. He owns a lot of properties. As soon as he sells one, he buys another. He lives in half of the city, his domain is vast and ever-changing. The Estate Agent worries about his time, he has everything planned out in advance, now he's going to rest for five days in a whole variety of ways, then he'll work for an hour and a half, then take three weeks off, then he'll go for a business lunch and fly off to the coast for a fortnight, and on and on it goes. The Estate Agent owns hectares of apartments, whole square kilometres scattered across various different floors in the city. He deliberately doesn't rent some of them out for a long time – he leaves them empty and walks around them with his hands behind his back like Napoleon and thinks about the time that has passed through these rooms. He is completely obsessed with time. He walks around his type 3672+2187 apartment, from which he will sometimes slice off a two-bed or one-bed apartment, or a studio flat where three philosophy students or fifteen Moldavian gastarbeiters will languish like mudpuppies. He goes through his numerous tasks – airing, letting the walls cool down. Everything is covered with the remnants of the occupants, remnants of the world they created between these walls: they've been gone for years but their remains still linger like severed roots in the rooms. All those dark deeds, the automated movements, the little paths and larger paths they trod, the millions of family dinners, millions of couplings, slaps, kisses, handshakes, smiles. Each space is infected with so many stories it makes you dizzy.

So we ended up in one of the Estate Agent's apartments and during my lecture on human loneliness – on the isolation that forced a horse to think – I drank half a litre of eggnog since there was nothing else to drink. In the meantime, everyone else has fallen asleep, apart from one young guy rocking in the corner, staring at a pool of rum on the floor which looked to have been spilt by Rorschach himself, and the guy had a tear-stained face and was confiding something to the pool.

You dropped off for a while too, Anna. You are breathing next to me, your hand twitching in your sleep. I stroke your hair. Evening is approaching with a faint rumble of thunder. A lark or something singing outside: treeookoo-treeookoo-treeookoo, how about that? Anna, wake up, we have to go. The Estate Agent is in the next room, showing the apartment to some potential buyers. He's threatening to sell us too if we don't get out. The party is moving on somewhere else, so we'd better leave. Before we reach the foot of the stairs, the rain comes on, big heavy drops slamming into the ground, splattering into the dust and the hot slabs of the pavement. You can smell the asphalt. I quickly flag down a taxi. The salt-of-the-earth driver opens the door and resets the meter.

'Where to?' he asks, and I tell him truthfully that I don't know.

About ten of us squeeze inside, some of my old friends the IT experts, the young guy completely soaked from hugging his pool of rum, two female anarchists in love. All of them screaming and bawling, arguing about art, politics, and God. Someone has a TV on their lap so our friend the Entertainer can be with us too. Through a crack I catch sight of the Estate Agent in the boot, deep in conversation with a barely adult big-eyed doe. The taxi driver has put the car in gear and now we are speeding through the evening into the depths of the city. I hold you on my lap, you rest your chin on my shoulder and watch the torrents of rain. Blurred traffic lights and brake lights run in liquid walls all around us, the rain breaks umbrellas and rips cobblestones from the pavements. But it is soon over. The storm has moved on like a five-kilometre noise. We drive on aimlessly. Along the roadside streetlights and billboards and neon poles are lighting up, a guy at a petrol station is flapping his hands as if to fan himself, shouting: you're still good, you're still good, stop! In fact, there's something going on all around us, mostly it's getting dark, the air is sizzling with the residue of electricity, everything has been washed clean and moisture is evaporating from the ground. Just like a year ago and a hundred years ago, the birds are squawking in the courtyards and there's so much I'd like to tell you, Anna, but I can't because someone has elbowed me in the ribs as they were trying to show how many people died during the Second World War. 'All of our problems are totally ridiculous in comparison,' shouts a puny nineteen-year-old director who's in the middle of filming his opus, *Hitler's Ward*, in which he is preparing to expose the roots of evil through the love story of a young Jewish girl who by a twist of historical fate becomes the lover of…and so on and so on. You can see he intends to put the whole sum of his life experience into this film, he's also studied a lot on the internet and perhaps in order to make this clear he screams: 'In Treblinka alone they killed 800,000 people!' One of the anarchists turns round, truly horrified, 'Jesus Christ, that's like someone murdering Slavoj Žižek's Facebook profile.' The Estate Agent is lying in the boot as though on a couch, holding a cocktail. While we were getting into the taxi, he bought it along with the whole bar and the block of flats where that crappy dive languishes. He sips sedately as he engages in a profound debate on the Big Bang with the doe.

Someone has turned up the TV they are holding on their lap because the Entertainer is talking on a programme called *Miracles of Civilisation*: 'A child was born in Japan, a bright healthy little girl. And she'd hardly had time to take in her surroundings before she began to laugh. She began to laugh at the age of eight months, and she has been laughing for fourteen years straight. She laughs uncontrollably from morning till night, even in her sleep, she can't do anything else, the laughter tires her out so much that she is barely able to get out of bed in the morning. She can't eat because the food falls out of her mouth, she has to be fed intravenously. The girl's father has spent almost all of his money on neurological tests, he's got into debt, but no one knows how to stop this laughter. And so they live together and at night they listen to the endless chuckling from the girl's room.' Signature tune. Footage from a demonstration calling for the internet to be considered a living entity and incorporated into biology textbooks. Then an intermezzo: a flippant song, a robotic band from South Korea singing about love and springtime.

Somewhere on the other side of the car people have started dancing as far as the space will allow, there's a party kicking off judging by the popping of champagne. Outside the world flits by, it's still there. I lower the window to let in some air. Anna, sometimes I miss reality. I miss you.

Darkness has fallen. I've covered us with the curtain someone pulled down at the Estate Agent's, curtain rod still intact, and put on instead of a coat, and while we are variously examining each other in our bunker, all shy and pressed together like two tennis courts – everything in us is so neatly aligned – the song finishes on the TV and the Entertainer comes on and says: a watchmaker in a Swiss town went mad – I know this from a reliable source. There is the rumble of thunder outside the window – we're stuck in the rainy season. And you are sweating a little and that is better than all of those games outside. Of all possible realities I choose yours. We cuddle in our half-sleep.

Night then, Anna.

Maybe we'll arrive somewhere tomorrow.

Žižkovite

Patrik Banga

Translated by Alex Zucker

I'M A ŽIŽKOVITE. A Žižkovite isn't just a person who lives in Žižkov or comes from there. It's a person who understands Žižkov as a place with its own rules, a place where everybody belongs and always feels at home, even if they haven't lived there in 30 years.

I grew up on Bořivoj Street, right on the corner of Bořivoj and Ježek, in a giant tenement house, back in the days when most of the people living in Žižkov were musicians, unappreciated intellectuals, workers, and Roma. A whole lot of Roma. Our building had only cold water, we kept warm using stoves fuelled by coal fetched from the cellar, the toilets were in the hallway, and we could only dream of having bathrooms like the ones we have now. From today's point of view, we were down-and-out. Back then, though, almost everybody in Žižkov lived that way.

When the coal ran out, we had to go down to the cellar to get it, which meant four flights down, then four flights up again with a full bucket. You might say that's no big deal, but try doing it when you're four! The cellar was crawling with cat-sized rats, so we would go down to the cellar in twos, sometimes even in fours. Luckily, we had enough kids in our family that we could do that. Plus, the whole building was dark. The only place where there was even a little bit of light was the hallway to the stairs, where the sun shone in through a purple and blue art deco stained glass window, casting colourful spots of light on the floor. I thought it was kind of scary, but it was the only light there was, since the lightbulbs never worked.

Outside the building's front door was where the world began. Our world, where it didn't matter whose kids were in our flat or whether I was over at some other family's place. We lived like true Roma: everyone together. In almost every building in the neighbourhood, we had an aunt who would feed us if we were hungry, or let us stay at her place and play with her kids. Old Mrs. Cínová baked bobaľki, Aunt Siváková cooked hot meals. We were friends with her daughters, Martina and Helena, who gave me my first kiss. A few hundred yards away lived Aunt Olina, and our grandmother's place was on Olšanské Square, where the whole Banga family would often gather. In short, Žižkov was our home.

One big advantage of Žižkov was the buildings were arranged in enclosed blocks, with little gardens or courtyards hidden away on the inside, where we could spend our time. When that wasn't enough, we would go and play on the field by the FK Viktoria Žižkov football stadium. I smoked my first cigarette there, a Femina. My mum beat me so badly I still remember it now, 35 years later. Other times, we would go scare the girls at the old Jewish cemetery, on the site where the TV tower now stands. Then, in the summer, we would head to Jiří z Poděbrad Square and spend hours splashing around in the fountain, a sculpture called United Europe, while the older kids went off to Rieger Gardens – our mum wouldn't let us younger kids go unless we were with her, which was mostly in the winter, when all of Žižkov went sledding there. To this day, I still have a vivid memory of riding downhill on my greased-up sled, heading straight for a hardboard figure of Krteček, the cartoon mole, followed by the unavoidable crash with the sled being destroyed.

The ultimate experience was when one of the grown-ups would take us kids to the now defunct Obzor movie theatre. I saw more fairy tales there than I can count, and my mum took me to every single one of the *Winnetou* movies. And Vítkov! The hill with the national monument to Jan Žižka, the fifteenth-century Hussite warrior who gave the neighbourhood its name. Our nursery school teachers used to bring us there every day. Plus, Vítkov had tennis courts, and on weekends my whole family would go and play tennis there. In short, we had all we needed right there in Žižkov: parks, gardens, fountains, monuments, culture, sports. Maybe that's why people call Žižkov a state within a state. If it had its own government, it could easily be a functioning republic.

When I was still little, I didn't perceive the divisions between us Roma and the gadjos. I think it was because we didn't have much contact with gadjos, apart from the musicians and intellectuals who used to visit my father, a musician himself. One of those intellectuals was Radoslav Dubanský, the actor and theatre director, who made the 'mistake' of attacking the Communist regime in one of his plays. In a show of appreciation, the authorities assigned him to a job in a boiler room where some of my relatives worked. It was only later I came to realise that from Bořivoj Street down to Kostnické Square it was mostly Roma, and up toward Jiří z Poděbrad Square it was mostly gadjos.

I didn't experience Czech reality for the first time till I went to primary school. There was only one other student in my class whose parents allowed him to be friends with me. He was Romani too. The other kids would talk with us as long as we were in school; once outside, though, they kept their distance. From their parents at home they'd hear warnings like

'Better not make friends with that Gypsy boy, it isn't right.' In effect, that lasted throughout my whole time in school.

As the times and the regime changed, people changed too. In 1990, white people saw Roma as partners, making revolution side by side with us, but a few months later our parents no longer let us walk down the street alone, for fear we'd be killed by skinheads. And we had the same fears as our parents. Wherever we went, we heard about – and more than once we also saw – how 'the skins' were capable of absolutely anything, even when it came to kids. In Žižkov, where up until then we'd always felt at home, all of a sudden the guards and the salespeople in grocery stores started to check our coats and bags, assuming we'd stolen something. The police started following us into parks and harassing us, and a lot of us suffered ugly beatings at the hands of officers. Žižkov began to be divided along colour lines. Every gadjo knew it was dangerous to go out alone on Kostnické Square after 10pm, and the same was also true the other way around. So, for instance, the Roma would get together outside the church on Vlkova Street, and the gadjos would sit on the red benches beneath the TV tower, where the Jewish cemetery had stood for more than 300 years. I still wonder who had the stomach to make that decision, entirely humiliating the ancestors of the Jewish people buried there. How many people realise when they walk along Wenceslas Square that they're walking on pavement made from Jewish gravestones? The Communists launched their liquidation of the cemetery in 1960, then, over the course of my childhood, they completed this barbaric act. So now, instead of visiting a site of respect and reverence, we watch TV shows beamed from there. Honour labour![1]

In other words, to each their own – only I didn't belong to either the Roma or the gadjos. For one group, I was too dark-skinned; for the other, I was too light. With Roma I played guitar; with gadjos I played football. My closest buddies were Martin Sartori and especially Tonda Novák. The Nováks' was like home to me. Even when I was a little boy, I called Tonda's parents by their first names. I had open access to their fridge whenever I wanted, they would take me along with them to their cottage in the countryside, and Tonda and I were constantly getting up to mischief together. I actually got into conflicts with my own community for defending gadjos when Roma wanted to beat them up. Like the Stojka brothers, who were notorious in Žižkov. My brother once ill-advisedly allowed the oldest one to borrow my guitar, and that was the last we saw of it. The middle brother liked to pick fights, and whenever he ran into one of my gadjo buddies I would have to fight on their behalf, since they were lacking in the Žižkov street education I had. And the youngest brother was a junkie, who didn't give a damn about anything, so he assaulted any- and everyone, until one day my older brother had to teach him a lesson.

But that wasn't the whole story. The Roma in the Karlín district thought they were better than the Roma in Žižkov. And the Roma in the Nusle district, who were mostly Olaš, were the worst of all. Whenever we had to go to Synek Brothers' Square, it was practically guaranteed that someone would confront us. And it always ended up in a brawl – even a knife to the kidneys, in my cousin's case. Not only that, but the perpetrator had the gall to come threaten him more in the hospital. As if we didn't already have enough problems with gadjos, we also had friction among ourselves. To be honest, I can do without the Nusle Roma. To this day, I still get a weird feeling that something's about to go down whenever I go to that square.

On the other hand, where else, except from Roma, could I have gotten such a solid education in music? After all, one of the first questions we always asked each other whenever we got together was, *What instruments do your kids play?* You don't even want to imagine the disgrace if you dared to answer *None.* The first time the band Khamoro performed on TV, with a young Jarmila Balážová hosting the show before she became a famous journalist, it was as huge for us as if Jaromír

Jágr[2] had turned out to be Romani. I spent years learning to play with Filip Surmaj, the keyboardist, both of us doing our best to emulate Stevie Wonder. Later on, when the Romani groups Kale and Bengas had a boom in popularity, I saw Bingáč, Miguel Horvát, and the rest of the musicians from our community on TV. But the highlight was the singer Věra Bílá, she was a phenomenon. She inspired us all to go full steam ahead, and eventually a lot of Žižkov Roma became respected musicians. They were all part of the crew who used to hang out outside that church.

Each ethnic group had its own thing. From gadjos, I found out about computers, learning the basics of programming and discovering my ambition; from Roma, I learned to play piano and guitar, and came to realise being a Rom isn't just about skin colour. It's about your thinking and way of life. I made it my life's task to search for a balance between those worlds – a task made all the harder when the principals of Žižkov's primary schools got together and decided to separate off most of the Romani students into the single school on Havlíček Square, leaving only two of us in the school on Vlkova Street: me and Monika Slivková.

The moment I tried to apply to secondary school, it became clear I wasn't going to have it easy. I wanted desperately to be equal to the gadjos, and insisted on taking the entry exams for gymnasium, which prepares students to go to university. The school counsellor laughed in my face. She tried to convince me that Roma didn't belong in gymnasium, and that even if I did complete my studies there I'd never get work, since Roma never lasted long in any job and they usually ended up in prison. She was so successful convincing me, I lost all my ambition and instead went to vocational school, where I studied to be a mechanic.

But the ways of the Lord are inscrutable. At age fifteen I met my first girl, and her mum, who was a journalist, showed me a different world, one where I could fully realise my potential. She brought me into newsrooms, and I got my first whiff of what journalism was all about. With her support, I got involved in a humanitarian project in Yugoslavia. From there, it was just a small step to a post at the Ministry of the Interior, where I worked with refugees, and an even smaller step to a job in media. I came to iDNES.cz a naive young man and left a respected journalist, headed for a senior position with Czech Television – maybe because there was no guidance counsellor there to tell me I didn't have what it took. She was wrong. Ultimately, I went to a specialised secondary school, and graduated in computer networks, graphic design, and the Web. And God knows, once my daughter grows up and I have a bit more time on my hands, I might give law school a try. It's never too late for education – you just have to want it.

A lot of years have passed since then. I've lost contact with my buddies. Most of them I haven't seen in over twenty years now, and most of them aren't in Žižkov anymore. When flats in Žižkov were privatised, Roma couldn't afford them, and the property developers, the very first traffickers in poverty, took full advantage, buying up leases for peanuts, then selling the flats to foreigners and more affluent Czechs for a huge profit. As part of these 'transactions', Roma were evicted and moved to north Bohemia. The smarter ones emigrated to Canada, then later to England, where they now live in totally different conditions from the ones who stayed in Czechia. So when people wonder how the ghettos emerged in northern towns like Litvínov and Most, they should stop and think about whether or not it was worth it. A few individuals made an enormous sum of money, but a whole generation of Roma, and not just the ones in Žižkov, lost their homes and along with them the chance at a twenty-first century standard of living. After all, ghettos aren't exactly where most of our lawyers and doctors come from.

Žižkov has changed. I can no longer walk through the door and act like I'm at home with every family there. When

I walk the streets where I used to live, I don't recognise anyone. Only the buildings, the tobacconists, and the butcher's on Olšanské Square still remain. Gone is the cinder pitch next to the FK Viktoria Žižkov stadium, where every local football player got his start. It's been replaced by new buildings, modern and ugly. They look nothing at all like our old neighbourhood, where every building had its own set of stairs, beautiful, decorative handrails, frescoes on the ceilings, and those gorgeous purple and blue mosaic windows. I don't hear musicians anymore, playing evenings outside the church, and I don't hear our Roma girls, in groups of three, four, and five, singing so gorgeously.

The magic has faded. No more harsh conditions, no more territorial battles, everything that made Žižkov Žižkov is gone. Kids don't go to the Viktoria match with their dads on Sundays anymore. Instead they play football on PlayStation.

But we, the true Žižkovites, carry the old Žižkov with us wherever we go. The place where we learned to share everything and that everyone has their place. We know how to hit hard when that's what it takes. And though everything disappears in time, just like the old Jewish cemetery, we will always remember our state within a state. Our home.

Notes

1. 'Práci čest' ('Honour labour') was a greeting widely used in Communist-era Czechoslovakia.
2. Jaromír Jágr (born 1972): a Czech professional ice hockey player.

Waiting for Patrik

Veronika Bendová

Translated by Paul Kaye

I GET UP IN the morning, quite early, and miss the tram. Raging.

Patrik has been in England since yesterday, at the Tomins's.

I think about what he might be up to as I head to the kiosk at Prague Uprising Square; I need to buy tram tickets, for myself and for the dog. I never know where to look: on the right, the newspapers, with all those awful headlines and images from the war in Bosnia; and on the left, from top to bottom, surrounding the spinsterish fifty-something behind the counter, hang the dirty magazines. It's embarrassing to look at them, but those big bulging breasts just draw the eyes.

'A couple of two-crown stamps and one four-crowner,' I ask the woman.

'We don't have any four-crown stamps,' she says.

'Four two-crown ones, then.'

Oh my god, what am I saying! Stamps? I wanted tram tickets! An understanding smile: 'No problem, miss.' The tram arrives; I just hope no one is sitting in *my* seat. It stops and I look inside apprehensively. My fears have been realised! Some foreign lout in the seat behind the driver. *What gall,* I think. How can he not see that this seat is for people with dogs? And the tram is almost empty. I push the dog ostentatiously into the place at his feet, but of course he just carries on sitting there. What if I were to fall? But it's all pointless.

I sway in the tram, tourists tread on the dog; I get out at Pohořelec. Five minutes past half nine; if Martin's already at the shop there'll be words.

At the shop Ota is sitting smoking nonchalantly, tapping his ash into an ashtray in the form of a misshapen woman (Japanese, revolting, circa 1920, catalogue No G 567, price 850 crowns; can be discounted). Which means Martin isn't here. As usual, Ota is wrecked. 'Veronika! Veronika!' he says. 'I'm so exhausted!'

Tie the dog up, put the speaker cabinets out, plug in the amplifier, put the book table against the wall, hang up the postcards, put the keys away, re-check the till.

Console Ota, reattach a map that's peeling off the wall, brew coffee, put fresh water in the vase. And now here come the people.

'Guten Tag! Bonjour, Hello, Danke schön, Gracias, Prego! Do come again.' I can't stand foreigners!

At half one, Roman Džupinka comes by, takes Beastie out for a walk, has a coffee, changes his T-shirt, sells a map and a picture of Prague; he's a bit slack to be a sales assistant. 'Why did you give her a name like that?' he asks, rubbing Beastie under the ears. 'I mean, she's a midget.'

'Well, I wanted a black German shepherd, or a briard, or at least a big schnauzer, but they offered me Anička here and she looked up at me with such sad eyes. And I knew she'd get through a lot less grub too!'

'Anička?'

'Well, that's what they called her at the dog shelter.' Džupinka laughs, but he can't talk when it comes to names, since probably no one else in the world has the surname Džupinka, apart from his old man, who left them – him and his disabled mum and his little sis – to struggle away in a two-room flat on an estate in Řepy. I'd never seen such a small flat until I visited Džupinka's place. Our mum and dad's flat near Charles Square is a hundred square metres, which I'd always thought was normal – until I went to the Džupinkas', at which point I realised that people didn't live the same way, even back in communist times; that a sick mother could lie on a couch all day in a single, sixteen-square-metre room; that such a space could double-up as a living room and dining room too; that a kitchen could be windowless, and just occupy a corner of a larger room, constantly smelling of burnt oil. Roman lived in the one other room, a mini-room, practising his viola all day so they wouldn't throw him out of the conservatory. He shared it with his sister, who was at nursing school.

Meanwhile, Roman inspects the shop. 'Why do you have bog roll and toothpaste out the back?' he wonders aloud in that dopey way of his. I explain that there used to be a chemist's here and they let Martin open a shop selling old maps and prints provided he kept a range of household supplies for the locals.

'That's weird,' Roman laughs. 'Baroque maps alongside Ariel and Vizír!' On my second date with Roman I took LSD for the first and last time. Now he is off again: 'Well, ok, bye pumpkin,' he says. 'Call me sometime, we'll go out on the lash.'

At half three Martin arrives with three boxes of merchandise. 'Ota, sort through this out the back; what are the takings like? And please don't tell me you've been smoking.'

Martin leaves again. Half five: count up the till, even out the discrepancies, chuck a customer out, answer the phone: 'No, Doctor Horký isn't here: he was earlier, but he left.' I count the last of the coins and the till is fifteen crowns short. I count again to be sure, and this time I'm two thousand and fifty-three crowns over. I count again, and then one more time. The small change varies but the two thousand is still there. Years of experience tells me that when you're two grand over somewhere, you're three short somewhere else; I stuff the excess into an envelope, write the amount on it, don't tell the boss, and slip it in the till; let's hope it'll sort itself out somehow tomorrow. Ota counts the cash in the safe out back, swigging on a bottle of pilsner, feeling sorry for himself, combing his hair. I get the dog, my bag and the keys. The phone rings.

From the receiver a meek and patient voice introduces itself as a Mr Lahovec. I remember putting aside a religious etching and three wretched portraits of saints under that name: Mr Lahovec gives the unmistakeable impression of being a cleric. A cleric who wants to go on a date with me. In all propriety, the meek voice assures me quickly. 'He was here in the shop,' Ota tells me now, 'and asked what the young lady likes to read: does she like surrealism, perhaps?'

'You know,' says Mr Lahovec into the phone, 'you were so kind to me I promised myself I'd do something, and I'd like to honour that pledge to you.' I promise him an hour after work tomorrow.

I'm excited; I've never had any dealings with churchmen. I'll have to think who I can tell about it! Ota turns the lights off and gives me a book – a slim volume with a large number 8 on the cover. 'It's from Martin,' he says; I look at the cover and read *Konrad Lorenz: Eight Deadly Sins*. I don't open it, just slip it in my bag, lock up the shop, untangle the lead from around the dog's leg, turn at the corner of Úvoz Street, and the whole of Prague lies before me. It's an August evening, the hordes of foreigners have dispersed, the city is infinitely beautiful. I will never pass up the chance to take in this view.

Ota and I are sitting at the Black Ox pub on Loretánská and the waiter is grumpy. 'Beer?' he asks, menacingly: two marks go on his paper; our Sparta cigarettes and a lighter come out; and the waiter is back already, hurling two glistening half-litre mugs on the table; the glasses thud against the table-top, and now there's just beer and foam; the best beer I've had, in the pub that's been serving it for 315 years.

Then it's the tram again: foreigners, Czechs, drunks, Beastie asleep and the driver taking no prisoners. At half seven I'm in Pankrác; above the church, the sky is on fire; I pass the third, fourth, fifth block and I'm home.

Mum calls; she and dad are at the country cottage and are making currant jam; she's calling from the neighbours' house, the ones that have a phone, and asks if I've remembered to water the plants at their place. 'Especially the bonsais, you know, they're in such a shallow tray, they can't be allowed to dry out in this heat!'

'No, I didn't forget!' What a liar I am.

Change the dog's water, put a bit of spread on some bread for tea, clean the toilet, count my cash, clear up the crumbs, go to sleep.

Before falling asleep I swear solemnly I'll go and water those plants tomorrow.

I get up, quite early, wolf down breakfast, walk the dog to the tram. Today just make sure to say tickets and not stamps! And don't let that tram get away.

'A couple of two-crown stamps and a four-crown stamp,' I say to the kiosk woman ensconced among the breasts.

'We don't have four-crown ones, so I'll just give you two-crown ones.'

'Sure, four two-crown ones, then.'

I stare at the postage stamps, pause, then hurriedly apologise. Unbelievable! 'Sorry, I meant tram tickets.'

'No problem.' But it is a problem! Why stamps? What is it I want to write to someone?

I run out, hear the tram coming, jam the muzzle over the dog's snout. 'Stop acting up, Beastie!'

I jump on the tram at the last second. There are some bags in the place reserved for dogs! And some old biddy sitting there, legs stretched out spitefully, gazing vacantly out of the window, *on purpose*!

So now I'm standing over a guy who reeks of Becherovka and I start to feel ill. Just after leaving school I got so rat-arsed on Becherovka with Ota that I spewed up in the bushes at Smíchov station, and since then I haven't been able to stand the smell of the stuff. I'm glad to leave the pong behind when I get off at Pohořelec.

Ota is already at the shop, sprawled over his chair. 'Did you know it's our anniversary today?' he says. 'It's been exactly a year.'

I quickly think what might have happened a year ago and it takes me a while to remember; it's weird how things we used to attach huge, almost sacred, significance to fade in importance; was that unforgettable night a year ago really so unforgettable?

'Oh yeah, of course!' Awkward display of enthusiasm, indulgent nodding; turn on the lights, plug in the speakers, hang out the postcards, avoid Ota's gaze; but he speaks anyway.

'So we should celebrate it today,' he says, softly.

I feel shame; I smile and nod. Then I remember I've got that date with the cleric.

'Oh yes,' says Ota, disappointed. It's true that a year ago we were pretty happy, and close; now a year has gone by, and a whole load of things have happened. Best not to talk about it.

What about the till? I think. I look enquiringly at Ota. He pauses, then shrugs. 'How much is in there? Two thousand? OK, then just leave it for now; if need be we can write it off against some merchandise or put it in the *Colla russica*.'

The *Colla russica* is a drawer at the back of the shop, among the chemist's paraphernalia; it's where we put the money for things like cash-in-hand payments to sales assistants.

At half ten Martin arrives and sends Ota off to the Black Ox with a big jug for some beer. The sun is climbing higher, it's still morning and a tropical heat is developing. Martin has brought fruit from his garden, and fresh flowers. He brews coffee. Yesterday the takings were pretty good, so for once I'm not being told to get down to work. I put some Gregorian chant on the speakers, Martin in the back puts on Radio Golem; in the space between the two there's a schizophrenic mix.

See off some garrulous Italians, straighten the books outside in the tub, put up a poster, replace the water in the vase, break a picture, confess guiltily, Dr Horký briefly peeved; all swept away by Ota arriving with eight litres of beer, that superlative beer from the Black Ox.

By the afternoon it's already unbearable in the front of the shop; mop brow, smile sweatily at sweaty tourists: 'No, we don't have public transport tickets'; 'the Loreta Chapel? Head to the right.' Surreptitiously polish off a few ounces of Vlašský salad, resist the dog's pleading looks, reattach the map, chase a wasp away, straighten the books up, accept one beer, decline a second.

It's hot, hot, hot, and the till is still over by that two thousand.

The phone rings. 'Veronika!' Martin calls from out back. He's getting spirited after three beers. 'There's a Mr Lahvon or something on the phone for you.'

Mr Lahovec apologises plaintively: something has come up. So if I were to have time on some other occasion, he'd try to find the time then…

'So we *are* celebrating today, then,' I tell Ota in resignation: the churchman doesn't have time. Martin bellows from out back: 'He's no churchman; he's an engineer of some kind, isn't he?'

A huge disappointment, naturally. I remember I have to thank Martin for the book. He nods and starts pounding on the typewriter with unusual vigour, replying to some letter or other.

I sit down out front and open the Konrad Lorenz.

A thousand screeching Italians pile into the shop. Just what I want right now. I jut my chin out defiantly.

The Italians yield takings of four and a half thousand. Ota clasps me to his chest and lifts me in the air. We laugh like madmen and Ota goes for another batch of beer.

We leave work slightly addled.

Now we're on Myslíkova Street, in the Depreso café; Beastie is asleep under the table, Ota is getting mildly morose; he's stayed on the beers, I'm drinking one coffee after another. 'So this is where I ordered that second litre of wine a year ago,' he remembers.

'I was pretty squiffy by then too,' I add. 'But a year has gone by, let's not be getting down about it!' I tell Ota firmly.

We leave, it's around midnight, Ota staggers around, and then we're lying next to each other, fully clothed, in the bed in my parents' flat, listening to The Brontosauři; everything's just like last year, only this time it's Ota opening his heart up, and *me* that has to comfort *him*; he's weighing up the whole of the last year, thinking back, pointlessly, to what has passed, long ago, never to return. He grows sad, he sighs; I want to feel sorry for him, but I'm not able to. I think about how people can come to hate, to scorn, the qualities they once loved in someone.

Then Ota turns to me and asks about Patrik: 'All good?' He's asking genuinely, I know; there's no ulterior motive. I say something back and he says: 'Patrik really loves you so, so much; and I really, truly hope it works out for you both, so you can be happy!'

I realise that I like Ota. Differently to a year ago, differently to six months ago; he doesn't deserve even the slightest amount of scorn just because he hasn't been able to take what happened to him without wallowing in self-pity.

We say goodnight. I think of Patrik. I remember that I haven't watered those plants.

At half seven I slap the alarm clock, calm Ota down, take the dog for a walk, buy rolls for breakfast, cheese, veg.

I put the kettle on for tea, bring the washing in from the balcony. Then I get the watering can and finally go and water those poor plants. The bonsais, remarkably, are still alive.

I travel to work without a ticket and arrive late. Ota is off somewhere looking for stamps and some new stuff for the household goods section. The phone rings and Martin is fuming, asking where we've been. I say Ota has promised to be in by eleven. 'Make sure he is,' Martin growls. 'Call me before you leave this evening, I won't be in today.'

I count up the till, carefully, several times, and now we're no longer two thousand over, but just a thousand. I count again and again, but the fact is there are two five-hundred notes fewer than there were yesterday. I sink into despondency, then anger; Ota should have been here ages ago: who was it who said we had to get the till in order?

It's now half twelve and Ota is still nowhere to be seen, I'm on edge and doing totally unnecessary tasks. I never want to work with cash again!

The phone rings and from somewhere in the distance comes Ota's whining voice. He's describing his exhausting traipse around the shops: '...then I had to get a beer, then I fell asleep on the tram... Look, Veronika, I'll be in by...well, definitely by five. Hey, you've haven't forgotten we're going to the cinema today, have you?'

'No, I haven't!'

'You're not angry, are you? Look, OK, Veronika, today's money is all yours; I wouldn't have been doing anything much there today anyway...'

Serve a Dutch couple, read a bit of Konrad Lorenz, dust down the shelves, smoke a Marlboro in front of the shop, turn the cassette over, sell two tubes of toothpaste and a roll of bog paper, count up the till; a thousand crowns down.

At three I close the shop, take a twenty-crown note, walk

the dog to the delicatessen at Pohořelec and buy a hundred grams of Vlašský salad and a couple of rolls.

The shop assistant is pleasant, but only to me, because she knows me; to the tourists she stubbornly insists on speaking Czech, and when they don't understand she just speaks louder and rolls her eyes. But I can't talk: my German is pathetic and my English even worse. Martin has been teaching English for twenty years, so he makes fun of me and deliberately translates trifling things into Czech, like when he gave me that New Year card that read *Wishing You Much Light in 1993*.

Now it's evening and Ota and I are sitting at the 64 U Hradeb Cinema.

How I love that cinema! Because the way into it leads from Mostecká Street through a passageway, and it's so totally, beautifully retro, even though it's only from the sixties. And it's where I first saw that film *The Doors* with friends from school; I came home a bit sloshed and went on to my mum about Jim Morrishon instead of Morrison.

We also smuggle Beastie in; I've got her hidden in the bag over my shoulder and I throw my black sweater-jacket over it, so the usherette doesn't notice. And Beastie is really well behaved; she knows she has to be quiet, so I just stuff her under the seat; she sticks her head out between my legs occasionally, but the rest of the time just lies under the seat, giving off a bit of a smell: perhaps some poo got caught on her tail.

I tell Ota about the first time I went to the cinema with Patrik; that we weren't going out at that point and I wanted to see a film about drug addicts, because I was really interested in drug addicts, but I didn't want to go on my own, so I called him because I knew he was a film nut. And so this film starts and it was weird, there were no junkies, just some debauched murderer, and he's on a killing spree in a supermarket; so I spent half the film with my eyes closed and my ears covered, because I hate violent scenes, and in this one they were wringing out towels full of blood. Ota stares at me in puzzlement and I explain that I basically got the names of the films mixed up, the one about the drug addicts had 'steel' in the title and this film was called *Blue Steel* and it was about a mass murderer! Ota laughs wildly; I elbow him and tell him not to embarrass us as the film's about to start. But when I think about it, Patrik and I would probably not have started going out otherwise: what made the biggest impression on him was this girl inviting him to the cinema to see a film like that!

It's strange, sitting in a cinema with a guy you're not going out with. I suddenly think I probably won't be able to tell Patrik about it when he gets back from England, because he might be cross that I went to the cinema with Ota. He takes these things too seriously, perhaps because he's Catholic (I told everyone about that straight away, with a laugh: that I was going out with a Catholic), and he gets jealous.

I talked to him about what happened with Ota a year ago, I told him about it because it was pure and innocent; but it doesn't seem that way to him, so now I prefer not to talk about Ota in front of him.

Ota falls asleep before the end of the film; he drives me mad! Ota's asleep, but poor Beastie is shaking; maybe the loud noises are making her jittery. Taking her home first would take so much time, though, and anyway, when she's at home she just barks all the time, because her last owners tied her to a tree in the forest, and when I brought her home from the shelter I couldn't leave her alone in the house because she howled for days and gnawed at the doors. I just don't know what I'm going to do with her when I start going to college in September. But it's a school for creatives, so maybe they'll let me bring her into lectures, though I'm pretty worried that it'll quickly become clear I have no talent at all, that they made a huge mistake in giving me a place.

After the cinema we go home, in opposite directions: Ota

to Barrandov and me to Pankrác. We part at the number 12 tram stop on Malostranské Square. It's still a nice warm summer, there are loads of people everywhere; I just wish they hadn't given the Malostranské café that hideous English name – it's *criminal*! I walk across Charles Bridge to catch the 18, and even this late in the evening there are still a good number of people on it. Halfway along the bridge sits a lad with a guitar, playing Žalman's *Každý ráno boty zouval*, and almost against my will I stop and join him, and he lets me sing a whole verse myself, on my own, and to my surprise I don't get nervous, I sing well, even though it's so long since I last went to choir practice. Then we laugh together and I walk on, to the Old Town side. I'm feeling good, feeling happy; and this beautiful evening makes a poem start to form somewhere inside me. I don't have all of it yet, but it finishes like this: *Like a lit cigarette / summer's end comes yet.* And for a moment I don't think about how even this little singing episode on the bridge will probably upset Patrik, and that I'll probably not tell him about it. For a moment I feel light and happy; Beastie is padding along at my feet, the summer darkness is all around, and the pleasure boats from the rental place by the Žofín Palace are bobbing on the Vltava.

And it strikes me again, when I look across the river at Prague, that all of this beauty is here because war didn't pass through this way like it did in Bosnia; because we were cowards; because in 1938 we didn't defend ourselves and we let the Germans occupy us, because if we had defended ourselves, none of this would have been left standing: Prague Castle wouldn't be standing, maybe not even Strahov Church, or the baroque houses on the Malá Strana riverbank that are slowly sinking into the water; maybe not even the workers' cottages at Kobylisy, or the courtyard-balcony houses in Karlín, or the atmospheric Nový Svět Street; instead, in their place, there would just be high-rise prefabs everywhere, and Prague would be as ugly as bombed-out Warsaw or Berlin.

And when I picture that, I'm glad we were cowards, because Prague was worth it…

I'm on the tram to Pankrác; Beastie is sleeping, I'm smiling out of the window.

I'm happy, even though I'm going on twenty and I'm dreadfully old.

I'm happy, and I don't know that the 64 U Hradeb Cinema will soon be closed down, like dozens of other Prague cinemas; that Beastie will come with me to lectures and screenings at the FAMU Film and TV School, and that just after I graduate in 1999 she will die of mammary cancer.

I'm happy, and I don't know that Martin will have to give up the shop in three years' time, because it's not even covering its rent; that he will turn to drink and will leave his school.

I'm happy, because I don't know that Mum will be killed in a car crash four years later, or that Ota will jump under a train in 2002.

I'm happy, and I don't know that Patrik and I will get married and will be together for 27 years – plus who knows how many more – and that it won't be an easy marriage; that we'll have five children. That there will come a time when Charles Bridge will be deserted, even in the middle of the tourist season, that the whole of Prague will be totally empty, and that singing will be banned. That another war will come, just a short distance from us and as thoroughly monstrous as that last one.

That everything will be completely different, but that Prague will be as beautiful as ever.

Yes, I know that's corny, but I just can't help it.

1993-2022

About the Authors and Editors

Michal Ajvaz, born in Prague in 1949, is a fiction writer, poet, essayist, and translator whose books have been published in 24 languages. His many prizes include the Jaroslav Seifert Prize (2005) for the novel *Prázdné ulice* (Empty Streets), the 2012 Magnesia Litera Award (Book of the Year) for the novel *Lucemburská zahrada* (The Luxembourg Garden), and the 2020 State Prize for Literature in recognition of a lifetime's work of excellence. The novels *The Other City, The Golden Age, Empty Streets,* and *Journey to the South* are all published in English by Dalkey Archive Press.

Patrik Banga (born 1982) is a Czech writer, journalist, and musician. His memoir *Skutečná cesta ven* (The Real Way Out), about growing up as a Rom in 1990s Prague, won the 2023 Magnesia Litera Award, in the Discovery of the Year category.

Veronika Bendová (born 1974) has spent her whole life in Prague, where she is the mother of five. She studied film screenwriting and dramaturgy at the city's FAMU film academy. She made her literary debut in 2012 with the novel *Nonstop Eufrat*, which has been translated into Spanish. She followed this in 2019 with *Vytěženej kraj* (A Depleted Land), which shortlisted for the Magnesia Litera Award (prose category). She is currently editor at the Twentieth Century Memorial Museum.

Simona Bohatá (born 1965) spent her adolescence in the working-class Prague neighbourhood of Žižkov, which became the backdrop of her first novel *Máňa a my druzí* (Máňa and the Rest of Us, 2017). Her third novel *Klikař Beny* (Lucky Beny, 2021) was nominated for the 2022 Magnesia Litera Award.

Petr Borkovec (born 1970) is the current Poet Laureate of Prague. He has worked as an editor for various Czech journals and newspapers. Since 1990 he has published more than 20 books – poetry collections, short stories, and works for children. A selection of his poems in English translation, *From the Interior: Poems 1995–2005,* was published by Seren in 2008. His work has been translated into German, English, Italian, and Romanian, and he has translated into Czech the poetry of Vladimir Nabokov, Yevgeny Rein, Joseph Brodsky, Yuri Odarchenko, and others.

Irena Dousková (born 1964) is a Prague-based writer and playwright. Having graduated from the Faculty of Law at Charles University, she worked variously as a journalist, a librarian and a dramaturge at a cultural centre. Since 2006 she has made a living from writing books, dramas and film scripts. Her work has been published in sixteen languages.

Bohumil Hrabal (1914-1997) belonged to a cohort of prominant Czech writers and artists to emerge from the tight constraints of Stalinist Czechoslovakia to become, in the more liberal 1960s, one of the most prolific and popular writers of his time. During and after World War II, he worked at a number of jobs including as a railway dispatcher (as captured in *Closely Watched Trains*), a steelworker ('Larks on a String' among other short stories); and an employee in a scrap paper depot (*Too Loud a Solitude*). Collections of his stories began appearing during the pre-Prague Spring thaw of the 1960s, and from then on, he was able to make a living as a freelance writer. During the harsh period of 'normalisation' that followed the Soviet invasion of Czechoslovakia in 1968, he made an uneasy peace with the regime and remained in print.

Yet his best work, like the novel *I Served the King of England*, and non-fictional portrait, *The Gentle Barbarian*, could only appear in samizdat, or self-published, editions.

Ivana Myšková (born 1981) is a Czech writer and editor. She graduated in creative writing and media communication from the Literary Academy in Prague. In 2012, she published her novella *Nícení* (The Inflaming), for which she was nominated for the Czech Book Award and Josef Škvorecký Award. In 2017, she published a collection of short stories entitled *Bílá zvířata jsou velmi často hluchá* (White Animals Are Very Often Deaf), which was nominated for the 2018 Magnesia Litera Award and has been translated into Polish and Slovenian.

Marek Šindelka (born 1984) studied Cultural Studies at Charles University in Prague and screenwriting at the FAMU film academy. His debut poetry collection, *Strychnin a jiné básně* (Strychnine and Other Poems, 2005) won the Jiří Orten Award for writers under 30. His novels and short story collections have been translated into several languages, including English, French and Dutch, and have won two Magnesia Litera Awards.

Marie Stryjová (1931-1977) was born in Dembrovka, a Czech village in Volhynia in northwestern Ukraine (a region in which Czech, Russian, Polish and Ukrainian nationalities and languages coexisted), where she spent her childhood and early youth. In 1947, her family resettled near Broumov in northeast Bohemia, close to the Polish border, but lost all its possessions in the enforced collectivisation following the 1948 communist putsch in Czechoslovakia. In the early 1960s she began writing fiction, mostly short autobiographical prose set in Volhynia, the Broumov region and Prague, but none of it was published until after her death. 'Blue' is her first prose work to be translated into English.

Jan Zábrana (1931-1984) was a Czech poet, prose writer, and translator. Unable to complete his university studies because his parents were persecuted and imprisoned by the communist regime, he had to take up a variety of manual jobs before making his name as a translator from the English and Russian. He introduced Czech readers to such major authors as Osip Mandelstam, Isaak Babel, Boris Pasternak, Lawrence Ferlinghetti, Sylvia Plath, and Allen Ginsberg. Much of his own work was only published posthumously, with just three collections of his poetry appearing in his lifetime. After the fall of communism, Zábrana's diaries appeared under the title *Celý život* (A Whole Life) and led to a re-evaluation of him as a major Czech writer.

Jan Zikmund (born 1992) read English at Prague's Charles University and works for the Czech Literary Centre. He is an editor of the international literary magazine *B O D Y*, and member of the jury of the Magnesia Litera Award for Poetry, the most prestigious Czech literary award.

About the Translators

Alžběta Belánová (born 1977) left her native Prague at the age of 12 and lived in the UK and Canada before settling in the US, where she received her English Degree from Rutgers University and the Schaeffer Fellowship in Literary Translation from University of California at Irvine in 2004. Her translations have appeared in literary journals (including *Asymptote*), and in books published by Motto Press, and elsewhere.

Geoffrey Chew (born 1940) is Emeritus Professor of Music at Royal Holloway, University of London, and has previously taught at the Institute of Musicology of the Masaryk University in Brno. As a musicologist, he has specialized in the music of the Czech Lands and Slovakia. As a translator of Czech literature, he has published *And My Head Exploded: Tales of Desire, Delirium* *and Decadence from Fin-de-Siècle Prague* (2018), a selection of short stories, and Karel Hynek Mácha's *Gypsies* (2019).

Melvyn Clarke (born 1956) is a graduate of the School of Slavonic and East European Studies in London, where he studied Czech and Slovak language, literature, and history. Recent published translations into English have included: *Christmas in Bohemia* by Kamila Skopová, *The House Beyond the Mist* by Ester Stará, and *B. Proudew* by Irena Dousková. Since 1999 he has moderated Czechlist, an online translators' discussion forum, and he currently teaches Czech-English translation at the Belisha Beacon School in Prague.

Graeme Dibble and **Suzanne Dibble** are a translating duo from Scotland who have been permanently based in the Czech Republic for the past 16 years. As history graduates, many of their translations have focused on historical topics, but they have also translated a number of books about music and art and are increasingly making forays into literary translation.

Paul Kaye was born in Bolton in 1969 and, after studying biology and French at university, moved to Bratislava, Slovakia, shortly after the break-up of Czechoslovakia. While teaching English he began picking up the local languages, later moving into radio journalism and translation. He then worked for a decade as an environment policy journalist in Brussels, where he lives and now works as a translator for the European Union.

Andrew Oakland was born in Nottingham in 1966 and is a graduate in German from the Universities of Southampton and Nottingham. From 1994 he taught for ten years at Masaryk University in the Czech city of Brno, where he still lives. He has been a freelance translator from the Czech and the German since 2005. Novels in his translation include Michal Ajvaz's *The Golden Age* (a Fiction Finalist at the 2011 Best Translated Book Awards), *Empty Streets* and *Journey to the South*, Radka

ABOUT THE TRANSLATORS

Denemarková's *Money from Hitler*, Martin Fahrner's *The Invincible Seven*, Kateřina Tučková's *The Last Goddess,* and a new rendering of *Mikeš*, Josef Lada's classic Czech work for children.

Justin Quinn was born in Dublin in 1968 and is a lecturer at the University of West Bohemia. His translations of Jan Zábrana's poetry, *The Lesser Histories,* were published in 2022 by Karolinum/University of Chicago Press. He has published seven collections of poetry. His novel, *Mount Merrion,* was published in 2013 by Penguin Ireland.

Julia and **Peter Sherwood** are based in London and translate from and into English, Slovak, Czech, Hungarian, Polish and Russian. Julia was born and grew up in Bratislava, Slovakia, and worked for Amnesty International for over 20 years. Peter taught Hungarian at the School of Slavonic and East European Studies in London and in the University of North Carolina at Chapel Hill. Their translations include works by Balla, Ádám Bodor, Béla Hamvas, Hamid Ismailov, Daniela Kapitáňová, Ján Johanides, Uršuľa Kovalyk, Pavel Vilikovský, Petra Procházková, Noémi Szécsi, Antal Szerb, Krisztina Tóth, and Miklós Vámos.

Paul Wilson is a freelance writer, editor, and translator. As well as works by Josef Škvorecký, Ivan Klíma, Václav Havel, he has translated four books by Bohumil Hrabal into English: *I Served the King of England, Mr. Kafka and Others Tales from the Time of the Cult; All My Cats*; and *The Gentle Barbarian.*

Alex Zucker was born in New Brunswick, New Jersey, in 1964, and lived in Prague from 1990 to 1995, working for the Czechoslovak News Agency (ČTK) and the English-language newspaper *Prognosis.* His translation of Petra Hůlová's *All This Belongs to Me* won the 2010 ALTA National Translation Award, and his translation of Bianca Bellová's *The Lake* won the 2023 EBRD Literature Prize. He currently lives in Brooklyn, where he translates Czech and organises with SURJ NYC.